"No one here gets out alive."
- Jim Morrison

A DYING BUSINESS

First edition. February 27, 2023.

Copyright © 2023 Willow.

ISBN: 979-8215307434

Written by Willow.

For Amanda

(Don't Fear) The Reaper

"I am so disappointed in humans," Death said as he dropped his briefcase on the floor. The dogs came running up to him and jumped on his chest, saliva dripping from their mouths.

"Is that you, my love?" Death's wife called from the living room.

"Yes, my dear."

"Come in here and tell me about your day."

Death pushed the dogs off him, took his shoes off, picked up his briefcase, and walked into the living room where his wife was, placing his black hat on the stand as he walked past. Death's wife was sitting by the fire. She watched the flames with deep concentration while stroking Max on the head. Bruce and Jasper were lying in front of the fire now, soaking up its warmth. The only light in the room was the fire, and with the added floor-to-ceiling use of timber, the room felt like a log cabin.

"How was work, my love?" Death's wife asked, her brown eyes never straying from the fire.

"Dismal."

"Well, fix yourself a drink and tell me all about it."

"You know there was a time when the wife would fix the husband a drink," Death said, grinning.

"There was also a time when men died much younger," the wife replied with one eyebrow raised.

"Unfortunately, I know."

Death let out a sigh and pouted. His wife's comments reminded him of a better time. Since divorce became common and socially acceptable, humans no longer needed to poison and kill their spouses to escape a bad marriage.

"That time I remember very well. The business was booming then. Tell me, how many men do you think died from their wives poisoning their drinks?"

"Probably not enough," she replied in a matter-of-fact tone.

"Is that not how you killed your first husband, my dear?"

"Yes, it was. Alcoholism will always kill you, whether it be by the drink itself or a frustrated wife."

Death grinned at his wife in complete adoration, he then continued to the bar, loosening his tie as he went. From behind the bar, Death grabbed a crystal glass and an open bottle of Scotch and poured himself a drink. Death took a sip of the Scotch and felt so much more at ease the moment the liquid slowly trickled down his throat with a slight burn. He took his place in his favourite leather armchair, drink in hand and watched the fire crackle. The wife continued to stare at the fire. All three dogs were now asleep.

"So, my love, tell me what is bothering you."

"Figures are unfortunately at an all-time low. We are still experiencing a steady decline in turnover rates. According to the statistics, we are down one-million deaths from last year, which is astonishing considering the population has never been higher."

"What does Mr Sharp think?"

"He agrees that the figures are not great, but there is no real cause for alarm yet."

"Well, if Mr Sharp is not too worried, then I'm sure it is fine."

"Yes, but it's not *his* business, is it?" Death said, quite annoyed.

"No, my love."

The wife of Death was ever the calm and collected one. Generally, Death adored this trait which was one reason Death pursued her. However, this characteristic often meant that she sounded like a wise professor, and Death came across like a sulking schoolboy. Death supposed one of them had to be the passive one in the relationship. He could only imagine how horrid her ex-husband was to make such a peaceful person go to the lengths she did.

"I'm sorry for snapping, my dear. It's just that I do not know what to do anymore. If humans continue to combat fatal illnesses, I fear things will worsen in my line of work. I have to wait an average of eighty years now to collect. I remember the days when it was only forty years. Not to mention how much harder it is now to commit murder. The whole 'modern technology and going to jail' thing puts people off nowadays. I dearly miss the *Jack the Ripper* era. No prints, and the police were far easier to bribe then too."

Death sunk into his chair, feeling defeated. His wife turned to face him.

"My love do not lose heart. Humans will always find a new way to kill one another; it's one of the few things where we excel. Besides, if humans cannot find a way to end their lives, Mother Nature will come up with a thing or two. How is she anyway?"

"The same as me. She's trying to cull the ever-growing human population, but humans won't take the hint. She finds infertility they find IVF. She creates a disease; they create antibiotics. She says the only thing dying nowadays is the planet."

"Maybe you and Mother Nature could work together to find a solution?"

"Thank you, my dear, but I'm not quite that desperate yet. I think she is somewhat opposed to working with me anyway. She's all about balance, and I'm all about, well... the opposite."

"You know, I was reading the paper today about it being politically incorrect to call Mother Nature 'mother' because it gives her a gender."

Death laughed.

"Oh these humans. I'll never know how they think the real problem facing humans is political correctness. Never mind their planet dying; at least the public toilets are gender neutral. Their priorities are interesting, to say the least."

"Well, I don't believe it's something the poorer countries worry about."

"True. Famine is usually their concern... public toilets are a myth to them."

The thought of famine and third-world countries filled Death with happiness, but the moment was fleeting. Death let out another sigh, stood up and began pacing in front of the fire. His wife's gaze followed him.

"You know, I thought I had a winner when Mother Nature created cancer. Humans suffered from it for years without knowing what it was or how to combat the sickness. Then all of a sudden, doctors realised that too much sun and cigarettes are bad for your health, and they discovered chemo and radiation. Cancer is now practically useless to me... well except for those few religious people who are against medicine."

"My love, I do believe you are exaggerating. We still get plenty of deaths from cancer."

"Well not enough and certainly not like we used to. Cancer patients can live years with the illness before they croak and don't even get me started on the amount of people that survive cancer entirely," Death said pouting again.

Death stopped pacing and stared into the flames. His wife came up behind him, put her arms around his stomach, and squeezed.

"Cheer up my love; you are still the one thing humans fear most on this earth."

"Am I?"

"How could you doubt it?"

Death turned around to face her. Her eyes became menacing with the reflection of the flames dancing in her pupils. Death ran his fingers through her long black hair, stopping just after her breasts. He kissed her on the lips then he entwined her hands with his. Death pulled her along as he walked back to his armchair. Death sat down and enticed her onto his lap, wrapping his arms around her as she moved her nose up and down the side of his face.

"There have been times when I was not the most feared thing on earth."

The wife stopped moving her nose and looked, as if from a distance, into the fire.

"When?"

"When Stalin was at his most powerful or when Mao Zedong was in charge. Not to mention the old faithful - Hitler."

"My love, those leaders were just doing your work for you. Their lust for taking life made those men so powerful and menacing. Fear of death is fear of you. Nothing is scarier than you, for death is the only thing certain in this life."

Death smiled at his wife in complete awe.

"Has anyone ever had a better wife?'

"You've been around since the dawn of time, you tell me."

The wife's words had put Death at ease for now. He moved his hand so one was now gently clasped around the back of her neck. Death pulled his wife towards him and kissed her passionately. She kissed him back just as forcefully and bit his lip. Death then pulled away from her kiss and looked at her. She had a cheeky snarl on her face. He grinned at her with such esteem and lust as he carried her up the stairs toward the bedroom. There had been enough talking for now.

(I Can't Get No)
Satisfaction

"Why don't you and Mr Sharp discuss ways to make the death toll rise today? I'm sure the two of you can come up with something, and you must be productive about this my love. No more wallowing in self-pity."

Death was looking dressing table mirror, fixing his tie. The daylight streamed in from the windows making the white walls seem even brighter. Death could see his wife in the bed behind him. A single white sheet lay over her naked body. A true seductress and a match, even for him.

"I will try, my dear."

"Don't try; just do."

Death turned around and looked at her. Her hair was messy and her dark skin had a dewy look. He could see the tiniest trickle of sweat on her neck. The wife could tell her husband was enjoying the view of her. Last nights and this morning's activities had been quite the workout.

"Are you always so bossy?" Death asked her.

"Only on occasion, my love."

"Don't forget that I'm the powerful one, my dear."

"Do you feel like the powerful one?"

She pulled the sheet down, exposing herself. Death's eyes widened in excitement and if he were so inclined, he would have blushed. Death, like most men, was the same when it came to the nakedness of women. A slight giggle escaped the wife's mouth. She was well aware that she was the powerful one, at least at this moment. Even after centuries together, Death still found her the most beautiful thing on earth. She was even more breathtaking than a fresh corpse. Death crawled onto the bed until he was on all fours and hovering above her. He kissed her lips and her neck.

"You know the point of our arrangement was that you would be my devoted slave, yet somehow I always feel like I'm the slave," he said.

"I thought you wanted me for my mind my love?" She said almost snarling at him.

"Well, that... and your female charms," he said with a wink.

The wife looked at her husband lovingly but at the same time as if he was an idiot (a look many men have been privy to). She ran her hand through his hair.

"How is it that a man as great and powerful as you have succumbed to a woman?"

"I am sadly just like any other man my dear and, like all other men, I know that women are men's Achilles heels."

The wife laughed.

"Now I must go," he said.

Death kissed her on the head and then got off the bed. He neatened his clothes and put his jacket and coat on.

"What will you do today, my dear?" Death asked his wife.

"The usual, take the dogs for a walk, do some cleaning and then see what all those idiot politicians are up to."

"Have fun my darling."

"I will."

The couple blew each other a kiss, and Death walked out of the bedroom. He grabbed the newspaper, said goodbye to the dogs, and then was off. Outside, everything was utterly white, which contrasts Death's outfit of black on black. It was winter in the eastern part of the continent, so it was bitterly cold. The water fountain in the middle of the driveway was entirely frozen and snowflakes were falling from the sky. No grass could be seen. A sheet of snow had covered this part of the world. It was all quite majestical.

Death (if he was ever asked) would say that technically he walked to work but the building was literally next door. Death had built the headquarters in the very early days of his career. He needed space for paperwork as even Death himself was not exempt from that. There also needed to be a place where he could monitor the death tolls.

Death had found out early on that human beings did not like being dead for a reason he could not fathom. It seemed to him all they did was complain about how hard life is but when the time came for the end, they suddenly decided they liked living and did not want to die. He found this very odd and even after thousands of years of human existence, little had changed. In this, humans were consistent.

Death managed everything alone for a few centuries, but the human population kept on growing (while many other types of animals declined or became extinct). So naturally, over the course of time and death, Death needed to expand and hire staff to help with the running of the business. Death was very picky when it came to hiring people. Only certain people with specific skills were recruited by Death. They were given the choice of either the end or they could live (in a way) and become a worker for Death for all eternity. Many humans also made deals with Death to give their life in return for the life of a loved one, but Death rarely encountered humans like this anymore.

Death looked at his headquarters and marvelled at it. It was large and black. The workplace was built first and Death had the house next door built once he met his wife. The wife always commented on the difference between the home and the office. One was tasteful and grand, the other looked like a morgue but, that was precisely how Death wanted it. Death was at the steps to the main door of his headquarters when one of his workers ran past him and knocked his left arm.

"Oh, I'm so sorry Mr D."

"Running late as always are we Aurora?"

"Consistent in life and death."

"Your mother would be proud."

Aurora gave Death a wink, and he winked back, even at her own funeral she was late; something about the hearse driver needing to pee. Death walked up the stairs of the building and went inside. The place was buzzing as always. Death's workers from the night shift walked past him with no emotion on their faces. The night staff honestly look like dead people.

"Good morning, Mr D."

"Good morning, Botan," Death said as he handed him his coat.

Botan took the coat and then made himself scarce. Botan had offered himself to Death about forty years ago to replace his wife, who was dying of cancer. Death agreed to the swap. Botan died and his wife lived. Death decided never to tell Botan that his wife had been cheating on him with the postman for the last two years.

Death walked over to Mary, the chief receptionist. Mary had been with the business since the American Civil War.

"How are we today, Mary?"

"Very good, thank you boss."

Death walked through the rows of office cubicles. The computer monitors were bright and the phones were flashing from incoming calls. Everyone was busy configuring data, watching the death toll or finding people that would give their own lives to save another. Needless to say, the team who dealt with the transfer of death from one human to another was a very small group that spent most of the day getting coffee for one another and playing card games.

Death walked up the stairs to his office. Death could see a curvaceous rear through the door to his office. It was Anne, Death's personal assistant; she was putting unwanted paperwork on his desk and wearing her incredibly tight, mini-black skirt again.

"Good morning, Anne," Death said, opening the office door.

"Good morning, Mr D," she said, turning around.

Anne had been in the business since the 'Black Death'. She gave her life to save her twin sister. Sadly, her sister took her own life one year later after being consumed with grief after losing Anne.

"How are things today, Anne?"

Anne was holding a stack of paperwork in her hands. She always had this pile with her; it never seemed to get smaller. Anne came across as a sexy librarian. Her lips were their usual shade of red which complimented her fairest of skin so well. She even had the slightly too big, black-rimmed glasses.

"Not too bad. There was a train crash in Germany which took twenty lives plus that flood in Queensland, Australia has now reached a death toll of one hundred."

"Excellent."

"Is there anything else I can get you, Mr D?"

"Yes. I need to see Mr Sharp please."

"Yes, Mr D," she said as she turned away to leave.

"Oh, and Anne..."

"Yes, Mr D?" she asked as her long dark hair was flung around with the rest of her.

"It's Ah Mo Ne's from human resources death day tomorrow; can we do something for that?"

"Of course, Mr D. Consider it done."

"Thank you."

With that Anne left and Death looked at all the paperwork on his desk. Paperwork was like a creeping weed in Death's office. It seeped out of the bookshelves and covered the many relics Death had acquired over time. It was a dismal sight. Death's gaze was caught by a candle burning on top of the filing cabinet, one of those scented ones Anne insisted on having in the office. Death looked at the paperwork again. Then he looked back at the candle. Then it was back to the paperwork. An idea sparked but he reluctantly decided against it, pulled out a pen, and started reading the first of many reports. Death blew out the candle to avoid temptation.

Death was looking through a report on the mortality rate in Ethiopia when he heard a knock on the door. He looked up and saw Mr Sharp standing at the door. Death gestured at him to come in.

"Good morning, Mr Sharp," Death said, rising out of his seat.

"Good morning, Sir."

"Please take a seat."

Mr Sharp sat down and Death re-took the seat behind his desk. Mr Sharp's glasses were slightly fogged up and Death noticed he was wearing the same suit he had worn yesterday. Death was under the impression Mr Sharp never left headquarters last night. He was truly Death's most valuable employee. Death had watched Mr Sharp when he was alive. He admired his skills and intelligence. It was Death who approached Mr Sharp when his end had come. He had all the qualities of a great general. Death was sure that Mr Sharp would make the perfect right-hand man. What Mr Sharp did whilst he was alive was a mystery to all that worked at headquarters; even Anne and the wife did not know. Death liked it this way. The great mystery around him kept all the other workers in line. No one even knew how old Mr Sharp was. He was younger than Death (as all are) but he was considered an original.

"What can I help you with, Sir?" He asked.

"Well, as you know Mr Sharp, I am very unhappy with the figures of late."

"Yes, Sir."

"I was airing my concerns to my wife last night, and she suggests that together, we could find a solution to the problem as I cannot seem to find one on my own and I cannot no longer accept the argument that the figures 'really aren't that bad'. I must... we must have results. I feel these humans are losing the fear of me which I cannot have."

"I see."

"You and I have been together in this business a very long time. I can hardly think of a time when we did not work together."

"Indeed, Sir."

"So, I'm sure between the two of us, we can find a way to increase the death toll and bring this business back to its glory days."

"I agree Sir. I have been thinking about this problem as I know how irritating it is for you."

"I appreciate that."

"The death toll is at an all-time low due to modern medicine, the lack of a world war, and the major advancements in homicide investigations."

"Fingerprints have been the death of serial killers," Death said, shaking his head.

"I agree Sir. We are also at a disadvantage as the average wait time for Death... that is you... is seventy-two years and that number seems to be rising," Mr Sharp stated.

"Correct. I almost said those exact words to my wife last night. The problem is obvious, the solution... not as much."

"This is why I need you to think back Sir, to a time when you and the business were at its most productive. A past experience could help here."

Death sat back in his chair and thought.

"Well, there have been multiple instances. Plagues have always been good for me; these modern-day hygiene standards have ruined so much. We were absolutely run off our feet during the Spanish influenza. I honestly think any time before the Soviet Union ended was a great era for business."

"Yes, that's very good Sir, but could you be a tad more specific? Can you name an exact era?"

"I can name multiple... the Black Death, French Revolution, Russian Revolution, World War one and two, American Independence War, American Civil War, the Khmer Rouge's totalitarian regime, and of course, The Great Leap Forward. If you want me to be person specific, I would say definitely when Stalin and Hitler were in power. Those two were the best when it came to massacres; business was thriving with them at the helm. Now, all we have are corrupt governments and people killing in the name of a God. Oh, but it is worthy to note all those religions that made mass sacrifices in the name of a God – the Aztecs were fabulous for that."

Mr Sharp nodded; a plan was forming. Death could see the wheels turning over in Mr Sharp's mind. Mr Sharp's entire energy and body language changed. The potential and the death were visible. There it was - the solution to their problem.

"I believe we have the answer then Sir, I'm almost embarrassed that I did not come to this conclusion earlier."

"Well, do tell Mr Sharp?" Death asked, with anticipation.

"You said that business was never as good then when a person like Hitler or Stalin were around, or a totalitarian regime, correct?"

"Correct. And we must also mention the women who have served me very well. Queen Mary the First of England and Countess Elizabeth Bathory were marvellous for business."

"Yes, of course, Sir. We must be diverse here."

"Well, society does demand it of us, Mr Sharp."

"Indeed it does. So considering all the high points of the business, I think it is clear what we need to do. We need to create a modern-day Hitler or Stalin, a Pol Pot – a Catherine the Great even."

Mr Sharp stood up and started pacing back and forth across the room. Death could tell he was excited, which was not an emotion Mr Sharp often felt. His face was becoming red and he now had a childlike smile across his face.

"When I was looking through the books, our highest numbers recorded mimicked exactly what you said. Whenever there was a plague, a dictator, or a war, we had our greatest losses."

"Which are our profits."

"Precisely."

"And as we know, Mr Sharp, usually when there's a war there's a dictator."

"We have the history books to prove it, Sir. So either we could ask Mother Nature to release another Black Plague on the world…"

"That's highly unlikely," Death said, cutting Mr Sharp off.

"I agree Sir, so the second option is to create an all-powerful, all-evil dictator. One who is capable of committing mass murder and has no regard for human life. I am not talking of a begrudged rebel leader or some Communist party man. We need someone who will bring the death toll up by one hundred percent and convince millions of people that this is the right, no, the only course of action. And of course, a war could be thrown in there too."

Mr Sharp sat down, slightly panting from excitement, and looked at Death. Death pondered over his suggestion.

"But how would we create this all-powerful and all-evil dictator?" Death asked intrigued but wary.

"Who better than us Sir? We have met them all," Mr Sharp said, with a cunning look.

Death leaned back in his chair, a smugness airing around him.

"True. I mean I regard myself as the biggest Dictator of them all."

"Still the fairest one in my view Sir."

"Thank you, Mr Sharp. Well, he'll have to be someone who is easily manipulated and has the greatest ego on the planet," Death said.

"Preferably no family or friends. We don't need a wife or some idealistic spawn of his telling him that mass murder is wrong," Mr Sharp concurred.

Death got out of his seat and walked over to the window. He looked outside and watched the snowfall. Mr Sharp came over and stood at Death's right.

"Mr Sharp."

"Yes Sir?"

"You are superb!"

Licence to Kill

"**M**y love, that's a brilliant idea," the wife said, as she hugged her husband.

She then proceeded to give him a kiss which turned into a slight bite as she could not control her excitement. Death gave her bum a little spank as she walked over to the bar to make a drink. She was always such a tease. Death took a seat in the lounge chair.

"You've come up with such a good plan my love, that I'll even make the drinks tonight."

"Thank you, my dear."

She poured the whiskey into the crystal glass and handed it to him.

"Cheers," she said, clinking her glass with his.

The wife used Irish whiskey for the drink tonight. The couple had decided that they detested any whisky/whiskey that did not come out of Britain. They took a sip of their drink. The wife positioned herself so that she was standing behind her husband. She leaned herself forward, and Death felt heat and breath near his ear. Her lips were practically kissing his ear.

"You'll get something else as well tonight, my love."

A small shiver rippled through Death's body as she pulled away from his ear. She was the only one that could ever make him feel alive. Death turned around to look at her. The light of the fire always made her look and act like a temptress, which she truly was. The wife took her place in the armchair on her husband's right, never taking her eyes off him.

"So, I gather you think it's a good idea?" Death asked, grinning.

"It's an amazing idea. I cannot understand why you and Mr Sharp did not think of it earlier, though."

"Me neither but I suppose because it has been done before. Actually, it has been done many, many times. Perhaps he wanted to find a new method instead of the one that never fails."

"You know what they say, my love - if it's not broke."

"Yes to be sure."

Death turned away from his wife. His lack of creativity on this matter made him ashamed and he empathised with Mr Sharp. He was beginning to think he was losing his touch after an eternity. People can often go stale if they stay in the same job for a long time. Sadly there was no replacement for him. He was all humanity had. Death considered civilisation lucky to have him but he felt that he may be somewhat failing them if he didn't mix it up once in a while. No one likes to be bored. But the plan was a classic one and Death did love a bit of nostalgia.

"So, have you found the right person for the job yet?" The wife asked.

"No, not yet. Mr Sharp, Anne, and I will start searching tomorrow."

"Very good. It's a smart idea to have a woman's point of view."

"Yes, my dear."

The wife was ever the feminist. Death put his glass of Irish on the coffee table.

"So, will you create a Hitler and convince him to wipe out an entire group of people? Or will it be a Stalin or a Zedong and have the dictator keep to killing their own?"

"You know, I had not thought of this," Death said looking concerned.

Death leaned forward and sat in a thinking position. There were two roads here, the question was which one was more likely to succeed? He pondered over the state of the world and the feelings among humans at the moment. Racism had not gone anywhere; it was just less socially accepted now. True tyrants still wiped out their own but it always annoyed Death the lack of loyalty the dictator showed their people. Death decided to take the easier path.

"I think I'll go with a Hitler. I'm sure there's a group of people out there who would happily wipe out another faction of people."

"I agree, I think you may even find you have choices with this path. Fill these people with enough lies, hate, and firepower and you will have yourself an army. Do you care which country you find this person from? Which specific group of people is chosen as the unfortunate?"

"No, I'm not racist."

"Nor sexist or ageist, my love."

The couple looked at each other and cackled.

"All humans are equal in my eyes. So my dear, what is the something else you had in mind for tonight?" Death asked, raising his eyebrow.

The dogs all got up and left the room. They were very intuitive creatures.

"WHAT WE NEED TO WORK out is the key characteristics a person needs to have to be an evil dictator that wants to commit mass murder," said Mr Sharp.

Anne, Mr Sharp, and Death were in Death's office. Death was sitting at his desk whilst Mr Sharp shuffled back and forth around the room. Anne was in her usual upright position with the never yielding pile of paperwork in her arms.

"Well, as you just said, Mr Sharp, they need to be evil. Plus I would think quite gullible so that they believe whatever lies we say. I would also think that we need someone who is incredibly arrogant. Someone who thinks they are really smart but is actually quite dim."

"So, a dim narcissist? Well, that won't exactly *limit* the search results," Anne said.

Death laughed at Anne. She had quite the sense of humour/ sarcasm when she wanted to.

"And lastly, if not most importantly, they need to be greedy. There has to be something in it for them," Mr Sharp said.

"Well, we can't pick anyone who is a Communist then, they're all about equality," Death said with a smile forming from the side of his mouth.

Anne let out a laugh. Death had made Anne laugh, and Anne had made Death laugh, and it was only morning. Death felt very pleased by this, he felt there was much fun to be found in death if you looked hard enough. Mr Sharp let out a half smile at the remarks, which was all you could expect from him. The comment about Communism made him remember all the ideologists he had come across in his time. He had concluded that most ideologists didn't understand anything about the human race, which was one of Mr Sharp's biggest failings too.

"I think we should choose a man over a woman," Anne suggested.

"Why is that?" Mr Sharp asked.

"I feel men are so much easier to manipulate when it comes to power. And unfortunately, society still prefers to follow a man to a woman for whatever reason."

Death chuckled. Mr Sharp rolled his eyes.

"Anne I can see why you and my wife get along so well."

Anne smirked at Death. Death personally never saw why humans deemed men so important, they died the same way women did. Still, he adored the way men went into battle and were ready to die for their country and loved ones. Death found it odd though, that nobody ever commended women on their bravery when it came to giving birth. Women dying whilst trying to bring life into this world was very profitable for Death for thousands of years. Death found himself cursing modern medicine once more. It was safe to say, Death liked men more as they were his best soldiers. It was women who were his true enemies. He worked so hard to bring about himself (Death, that is) and all they did was give birth to another living being. He took it, and they gave it. He found the whole process terribly inconvenient.

"I actually agree with Anne. Besides, I'm not entirely sure how many women we will have to choose from. Also, it would appear that women have a harder time when it comes to killing children, I would say men are not as... hesitant," Mr Sharp added diplomatically.

"To be sure, Mr Sharp," said Death.

Death did truly marvel at the idea that men did all this work for him and he didn't have to pay them or promise them anything. Of course there was always some that objected to the notion of killing. Death found it especially pleasing when *they* met an early end. They were the ones to look out for. Too many of them and you might just have peace. No, passivists had to be stomped out. They were not good for business at all.

"So, how do we find such a man?" Death asked.

"We can search in the living database for a politician that has the qualities we need and go from there," Anne suggested.

"Yes, of course, but I must admit I am not as confident in this database," Mr Sharp said, with intrigue.

It was rare for Mr Sharp to go into the living database, although it was far smaller than the dead database Mr Sharp was always amazed at how working in the industry of the dead somehow meant you had to spend so much time on the living. Anne on the other hand, was highly involved in the living database, but she was the young one on the team.

Anne walked over to Death's desk and dropped the large pile of paperwork from her arms. She then ushered Death out of his own seat. Death reluctantly got up and stood behind her as she furiously typed into the computer. Mr Sharp stopped pacing and watched Anne with anticipation.

"It's quite simple. You need to put in the details you're after such as sex and age. Then you can even filter it to put in your desired characteristics. The system will find a match or matches for a person or persons who fits your requirements."

"Well, we've agreed on a man who is middle-aged. University educated and is most likely overpaid. Oh, forget that. He's working as a politician; we know that's a guarantee - single, widowed or divorced. And as we said, gullible, arrogant, and not too bright but at the same time charming," Mr Sharp said.

"We can't choose someone who is already running a country, we need someone original, someone who can become the new leader of a nation. I want an individual hungry and lusting for power," Death stated.

"Not already in power?" Anne asked.

"Yes. We need someone fresh. Humans always go for that new person who promises them the world but never delivers. Also, a corrupt politician would be great and give us more choices than the ones with some morals. Oh, I did it again, they're a politician, morals will naturally be without," Mr Sharp said shaking his head.

"Can we find a Politician that's secretly in some group? Like the Illuminati or a closet Nazi?" Death suggested.

"Shouldn't be a problem, there are plenty of them still around," Anne joked.

"And we need to choose a country that has an election for its leader coming up soon."

"But how can we be sure they will win?" Anne asked.

"Oh, we can rig that," Mr Sharp said.

"Exactly. Stalin is one of mine, we'll ask him and get some pointers."

"It's about who counts the votes right Mr D?"

"Precisely Anne."

"You do bring up a valid point about the country, Sir. It is not enough just to choose a leader; we need a country that is in great emotional turmoil and is looking for someone to blame. A country that is in the position to commit genocide."

"I wouldn't alarm yourself too much there Mr Sharp. Mass murder has happened in so many countries that I'm sure it would be easy to have it happen again. It is not unique to one country. However, I agree the plan would work better in a country that is going through some unrest and intolerance right now. There are a few to pick from."

If the condensation in Mr Sharp's glasses would let up, Death could see the apprehension in his eyes.

"I see your point, Sir. However, I still have the concern this method has all been done before."

"Yes, I did express that concern to my wife but we concluded that mass murder never ages – it is timeless."

"Maybe it's time you brushed up on your world history, Mr Sharp," Anne said, trying to create a rise out of Mr Sharp.

"Don't forget who the group's senior member is, Anne."

"Isn't that me, Mr Sharp?"

"No, Sir. You are the leader, not a member."

Death pulled a smug smile – he liked this.

"I am seven-hundred years dead you know," Anne said, crossing her arms and pouting.

"Oh, so young, nothing on Mr Sharp," Death said mockingly.

Anne rolled her eyes.

"However, Mr Sharp, *you* are certainly old enough to know and remember that history has a way of repeating itself. Humans, as smart as they think they are, rarely learn from the past. Besides, this will be a great cover as politicians always do this."

"Murder or rigging elections?" Anne asked but then quickly blushed. This was a rhetorical question.

"This will not shock the humans at all. Many countries are used to mass murder and the others are used to reading about it."

At this moment Aurora walked in with three coffees.

"Oh, my gosh thank you!" Death said rushing to the coffee.

"Don't be so dramatic Mr D. I don't exactly think you need caffeine to function like the living."

"This is my attempt at identifying with them."

Anne rolled her eyes, but she secretly enjoyed the joke.

"We should ask for Aurora's view on the matter."

"Oh no, are you three arguing again?" Aurora asked as she handed Anne and Mr Sharp their coffees.

"We're just trying to confirm something, is all," Mr Sharp said sternly.

"Yes, Mr Sharp," Aurora said, blushing and looking down at her feet.

"Aurora, do you think society would find a large number of humans being killed by other humans out of place?" Death asked.

"Definitely not," Aurora answered swiftly.

"Excellent, that settles it then. Thank you, Aurora."

Aurora nodded and left the room. Death gave Mr Sharp an arrogant look. Mr Sharp let out a deep breath. Death seemed to understand humans better than Mr Sharp did, which was disappointing as he was a living human...once. Not to mention he had been dealing with them for thousands of years (not as long as Death, but still worthy of a mention). Human's inability to learn from mistakes made Mr Sharp feel like he wanted to identify as a non-human animal more and more. He was jealous and impressed by Death, who could read a creature that was not his own. Mr Sharp (along with all the staff) still didn't quite understand what Death was. But he didn't worry about it too much – Death was the employer, he was the employee, and that was enough for him.

"Are you still with us, Mr Sharp?" Anne asked, concerned.

"Oh, yes, of course,' he said, startled, 'but I do have a concern, Sir."

"You always have a concern, Mr Sharp."

Mr Sharp narrowed his eyes. Death grinned and then shook his head.

"I apologise. Please voice your concern, Mr Sharp."

"Would it not be easier, Sir, for you to kill a billion or so people by yourself? Instead of having to go through all this?"

"That's what I think, Mr D. You always seem to be coming up with the most elaborate ways to kill living beings instead of just well... killing them," Anne added.

Death nodded, "I hear what you two a saying, and it's a valid question. It would most certainly be easier but far less fun. I would also be upsetting Mother Nature and her precious balance and I would rather not displease her. Also, that's not exactly how it works. Trust me, there is a method to the madness. There can't be a sense of mystery around why so many people are dead. There needs to be some form of an answer, an explanation for the humans in line with what they think is plausible and acceptable, even if it is not the answer they want. It needs to look natural."

"Natural?"

"Yes. I can never deter outside the realm of natural causes of death like we just spoke about with Aurora. We don't want the humans getting suspicious now."

Death picked up a newspaper on his desk and started flicking through it.

"Look here; the pages are full of people dying. This is what humans read about or watch every day. War and death are considered tragic by many but somehow never too surprising. The tale of people dying is as old as time. Just another part of history for the kids to learn about."

"The kids?"

"Well, I think we've established that adults never learn from the history books."

Anne contemplated what Death had just said. It was incredibly bleak but true.

Death looked at Mr Sharp very coolly. Mr Sharp could see a slight sparkle in the eyes of Death. Sometimes Death seemed more alive than the actual living. Mr Sharp nodded at Death, and Death nodded back, and there was an understanding between the two.

"Natural and socially acceptable it is," said Mr Sharp.

THE SEARCH FOR THE ideal candidate was not the quickest of tasks. It was a surprise to the three colleagues and yet it was also of no surprise when they typed in the words 'arrogant', 'ego' and 'greedy', every politician on the planet showed up. They needed to drastically narrow the field. They decided to rule out certain countries.

"Now I'm not trying to insult anyone here but I don't see how a dictator could come out of Canada or New Zealand. They just don't have *that* quality in them," Death said.

"I agree Mr D. How about this one? Timothy Williams," Anne said.

Death read his description.

"No."

"Why?" asked Anne.

"He has red hair."

"Are you being serious right now?" asked Anne, quite annoyed.

"They crucified that Australian Prime Minister that had the red hair."

"I don't think the red hair was the problem. Besides, people love Ed Sheeran."

Death didn't look convinced, "hmm... there's always an exception."

"Oh, honestly,' Anne said as she threw her hands up in the air in frustration, 'we'll never find anyone at this rate."

"I know. I'm sorry, Anne. Why don't you go home, and we'll start again tomorrow?"

"You mean today?"

"What?" Death asked, confused.

"It's already four in the morning."

Death looked at the clock in shock.

"I'm so sorry, Anne."

"It's okay; we dead people have all the time in the world."

She pushed the chair back and got up.

"Why don't you take the rest of the day off?"

With a wink, Anne said, "I was already going to."

"You know an attitude like that could get you fired, Anne."

"Oh, I don't think I'm that lucky. Besides, you would miss me too much," she said with an arrogance and Death knew she was right.

Anne walked away with a skip in her step. She stopped when she got to Mr Sharp, who was snoring away on the couch, covered in a blanket of paperwork. None of the workers of Death needed sleep exactly, but they were all so used to it and most of them seemed to enjoy it. Many of the workers, just wanted the saying 'I'll sleep when I'm dead' to be accurate at least sometimes.

"What about him?" she asked.

"Leave him. He'll wake up eventually."

"Yeah, I suppose. Bye, Anne."

"Bye, Mr D."

Anne left the room, closing the door ever so gently. Mr Sharp continued to sleep on the couch. Death could hear the birds outside. He kept on looking through the candidates. Slowly his eyes became heavier and heavier. Humans were not the only ones who enjoyed sleep. It was one of Death's favourite hobbies. He did not dream exactly but when he slept it was finally calm and quiet, just as death was for the truly deceased.

DEATH EVENTUALLY WOKE up to the sound of the telephone ringing. It was ten in the morning and the office was up and running. Daylight was streaming in through the windows. Death reached over and answered the call.

"Hello?" Death's voice was so cracked that it sounded like he was drunk.

"Thanks for the call to tell me you weren't going to come home last night."

Waking up to the voice of an angry wife was not the first thing he wanted to hear in the morning.

"I shall punish you for it when you get home," she continued.

"Yes, dear."

The wife's punishments were usually quite enjoyable and had been known to involve a red leather whip; however, more often than not, it meant doing the dishes or vacuuming.

"Oh, and you can thank me later for my help."

She hung up.

"Help with what?" Death asked confused.

Death looked around the room. Mr Sharp was no longer snoring on the couch and Anne had just walked through the office door practically beaming. Death turned to look at his monitor. And there he was, the perfect candidate. The wife was brilliant!

Welcome to the Black Parade

"**M**ay I present to you Mr Douglas Roach," Anne said.

Death stared at the screen and took in the human that was displayed before him. Mr Sharp had joined his colleagues in the office now with a fresh suit on and smelling of cologne, so it was assumed he went home and showered at some point. The three colleagues crammed around the computer screen, looking at it as though it was their firstborn.

"Your wife has quite the eye. He's perfect for the job, the easiest to manipulate human if ever I saw one," said Mr Sharp.

Douglas Roach was a forty-year-old Congressman for the Pavian party from the country of Urit. From all accounts, he seemed like one of the worst politicians ever to get a vote (which was saying something if you look at politicians). He had never been married and barely had a dating history. He was born in the capital of Urit (Uni Ted) and went to Trinity University. Douglas joined the Pavian party shortly after graduating. The only friends he made in university were rich with connections that helped progress Douglas' career. Scandals often surrounded Douglas - he had been questioned about cheating on his final exams, there was an investigation he underwent to do with himself and a street hooker, and he had rather a high gambling debt. All in all, he was tremendous for the job.

"This man is pitiful. I'm surprised he hasn't just killed himself yet," Death said.

Death noticed Anne had become stiff and tense at this remark. He swiftly moved the conversation along.

"I think the most important question is how do we get him to become the next Hitler?"

"You need to befriend him, gain his trust. You must seduce him in a way, we need him to fall in love with you or at least lust. If you do this then we can manipulate him to do practically anything as he will want to please you and will seek your approval on everything," Anne said.

"Is this what all women try to do to men?" Death asked Anne quite taken aback by her words.

"No. Not *all* women," Anne replied, grinning.

Death thought of his wife but decided to move on.

"But Anne, I must question the notion that he needs to fall in love with me."

Anne rolled her eyes.

"I think Anne meant it more in an adoration way, Sir," Mr Sharp added.

Relief washed over Death. Death had no problem with the gays of course – straight, gay or bi, dead is dead. And he would have it known that he did regret taking Freddie Mercury so young but that subject would be better taken up with Mother Nature.

"Oh, well in that case I'm all for it then," Death said.

"Glad we got that out of the way, Mr D," Anne said with a sense of judgement.

"But will Urit really get me the numbers I want? What is the population anyway?" Death asked ignoring Anne's tone.

"Fifty-five million."

"Well, that's not exactly China or India but it will do for now. So, what's the plan?"

"We promise him what all politicians want- we agree to fund him and support him to eventually make him the President," Mr Sharp answered.

"Wouldn't he question why some random person wants to help him become President?" Anne questioned.

"No, he's a politician; they really don't care about the legalities, reasons, and why's. They want the money and the power; an opportunity must never be wasted in politics," Mr Sharp said, matter of fact.

"I can't imagine why people don't trust them," Death said sarcastically.

"Should I book our flights to Urit?" Anne asked.

"Absolutely," Death said.

Anne left the room to go and book the flights with help from Mary.

"I'll go home and pack," Mr Sharp said, leaving as well.

Death put his hands behind his head and leaned back in his chair.

"MY GOODNESS THIS PLACE seems like the underworld, a home away from home," Death said to Anne and Mr Sharp as they walked along the banks of the main river in Uni Ted.

It was November, so the ugliness of Urit was in full in bloom. It was a cold day and the sky was the usual grey. Death had many memories of Urit. It was a country whose history was filled with turmoil. The country had been marched through by the armies of other nations many times as it was in a central location on the continent. It was taken over by Russians in both wars. There also seemed to be an odd number of plagues that had occurred in the country. It was quite a surprise that people still chose to live in Urit. You could practically smell the death as you walked around and Death wasn't referring to his own smell. Urit was not a rich or developing country, it was somewhere in between. If one was asked what Uni Ted looked like one would say grey and every street seemed to look the same as the one before. To be more accurate, most of Urit was grey. Life and colour did not thrive in this country. The only real beauty of the country was the large amount of forest that covered nearly forty per cent of the land.

"So, where is Government House?" Anne asked.

"Just up ahead," Mr Sharp said as he pointed to the distance.

"I don't want to judge a book by its cover, but Uni Ted is a tad underwhelming. Doesn't have the same significance as Moscow or Berlin."

"It is slightly humbler in appearance, Sir, but it will do the job just as well, I'm sure."

"I suppose. So, what am I meant to say to him again?" Death asked.

"Remember that all politicians are incredibly vain. You need to tell him how much you agree and applaud his politics and that with your help, he could become the next President. All the other politicians are wrong. He is the only one who can make this country great again," Mr Sharp said.

"What time was the appointment again, Anne?"

"Three."

"Lovely. Well, seeing as we have time, should we go grab some lunch?"

"You know this is one of those days that I'm quite happy I'm already dead and don't need to eat."

"What do you mean, Mr Sharp? I still love to eat." Anne said.

"I take it you have never tasted Urit cuisine, Anne?"

"No. Why?"

"Let's just say our death will not become it."

"I wonder if the hospitality is any better now?" Death asked.

As it turned out, it was not.

THERE WERE NOT MANY architectural designs in Uni Ted to admire, the only exception was the building the government was based in. It was quite a sight to behold. Instead of the usual grey of Urit it was bone white from the outside with a lovely garden surrounding it. Inside was a bit different. The building was built in the seventies and had not been updated since. The carpet was brown with beige and white swirls throughout, the walls were green and all the lights were yellow. The design of the building was quite unimaginative. It consisted of long, dull hallways with doors that opened into offices. There was a grand room at the back of the building where the government would meet, and a library in the right wing which was about it.

Anne, Mr Sharp, and Death all waited outside of Douglas Roach's office in some tacky leather chairs that smelt of mildew. Death was experiencing an unusual emotion, he was nervous. He wasn't sure if Douglas and Urit could pull off what the business was after. Anne quietly pondered over the lunch they had just eaten and wondered how anyone could mess up a basic steak sandwich.

Mr Sharp continued to take notes, for what exactly no one knew. Eventually a woman who they all assumed was Douglas' secretary stuck her head out the door.

"Mr Roach will see you now."

The three colleagues walked into Douglas Roach's office. The secretary stayed with the three to introduce them. Douglas was finishing a phone call when the three arrived before him.

"Mr Roach, this is Mr Black and his associates Anne and Mr Sharp."

Mr Black was the incognito name for Death. He decided on it sometime after the Black Death. Before that he used Grim, not to be confused with the Brothers Grimm, it was Grim as in Reaper.

"Thank you, Helen. You may leave us."

Mr Roach got up from behind his mahogany desk to shake hands. Death noticed how fine the suit of Douglas Roach was. Exceptionally tailored and the fabric was of high quality. Douglas Roach was an attractive man who was in great shape. Not particularly tall but he had a full head of hair and a luscious brown beard. His aftershave was a touch on the heavy side though.

"Mr Black, how nice to meet you," Mr Roach said as he shook Death's hand.

"Thank you, Mr Roach, the pleasure is mine. Mr Sharp and Anne are part of my team. I never go anywhere without them."

Mr Roach shook Mr Sharp's and Anne's hand. Death noticed a glimmer in his eye when he took Anne's hand. She had her iconic red lipstick on and a tight, black dress that made her look so fair and incredibly striking however Anne did not return the favour.

"Please, do sit."

Douglas took his seat behind the desk whilst the three sat on the other side of the desk.

"How may I help you, Mr Black?"

"Actually Mr Roach, I believe it is how I can help you."

Douglas looked intrigued.

"I'm all ears, Mr Black."

"Well, it's in regard to your politics and your way of thinking. I believe you have an excellent outlook for the future."

"Well...thank you," Douglas said, rather surprised.

"Let me get straight to the point Mr Roach as we are both busy men. I'm willing to back you, financially of course and with any other support I can muster, as I am confident you could be the next President of Urit one day and bring this country to its full potential."

Douglas was taken aback by the faith this unknown man had in him.

"Naturally, I'm very flattered. I admit it has always been a dream of mine to be President. But I'm concerned that I may have to sell my soul for this gracious support. This is not something I am offered on a regular basis."

"I assure you, Mr Roach, I am most certainly not after souls," Death said, barely containing a chuckle.

Death could see out of the corner of his eye that Anne and Mr Sharp were finding this all very amusing.

"Then what's the catch?"

"No catch, Mr Roach. I mean... we may make suggestions on your politics and actions now and then, but they will be in line with your own views, we swear to you," Mr Sharp said.

"We really are fans of you and your politics," Anne added.

Flattery was essential in politics – many arses needed to be kissed to get anywhere in this business. It was also easier to convince people a lie was true if it came in the form of a compliment. What Death was saying was music to Douglas' ears. The help from a third party could seriously elevate his career.

"How much of a contribution are we talking about, Mr Black?" Douglas asked.

"Pick a number," Death answered, grinning.

Mr Roach had a sinister look in his eyes.

"I assure you I can and will pick a very high number."

"A man's price should always be high," Death said.

Douglas hesitated. What was being offered was his dream, his goal. Douglas never considered himself a great politician, but maybe he had been selling himself short. Perhaps he had far more potential than he knew and the man sitting before him was the only one who truly saw it.

"Hmm... I must hesitate somewhat, Mr Black, as I do not know you or your colleagues."

"Well, we shall get to know one another."

Douglas Roach looked only partially convinced but the prospect of receiving unlimited funds without having to promise anything in return was very appealing to him. True motives would be revealed later and Douglas was sure they could not be too bad.

"We're sorry we cannot tell you more. We have to play our involvement very close to the chest due to... ah..." Death trailed off.

"Politics?" Douglas said raising his eyebrows.

"For lack of a better word," Death said, smirking.

"Have you spoken to Professor Wick lately, Mr Roach?" Mr Sharp quickly added.

Douglas looked at him, quite stunned.

"You were a student of his, were you not? At University?"

"Yes... you know him?"

"Of course, we have met many times. We initially met at a meeting for ah... likeminded people."

Douglas nodded. Professor Wick was a friend and ally to Douglas. He was also President of a club Douglas had joined back in his twenties. The club consisted mostly of males of a certain look and social standing. The members all believed themselves to be superior and the elite persons of the human race. Douglas suspected the three, well at least Mr Black and Mr Sharp, were also members of the club. Douglas would not be able to determine this for sure as membership was a sensitive subject, and the first rule of the organisation was the same first rule of *Fight Club* (you *do not* talk about it). The fact that Mr Sharp knew Professor Wick was enough to sway Douglas into trusting them. They were similar to him, which meant they could be trusted.

"I have heard of these meetings and these people. I have been to many of these meetings myself. I consider attendees of these meetings my kin."

"As do we, and we must always protect our kin and do what we can so that our family may prosper," Mr Sharp said, with a slight pout.

Douglas thought on this for a moment.

"I do not know you, but your views seem to be the same as mine, which tells me we share something."

Douglas' eyes darted from Mr Sharp to Anne and then to Death.

"I would be most gracious for your support Mr Black,' Douglas said, standing up and holding out his hand. 'Shall we all meet for dinner tomorrow night? I know a place that is half decent. Helen will give you the details."

"Splendid," Death announced.

The three shook hands with Mr Roach and then left his office.

"Well done on finding out about Douglas' involvement with that organisation," Death said as they walked down the stairs.

"Thank you, Sir. I figured we needed something so he would see us as a friend rather than a foe."

"But who is Professor Wick?" Anne asked.

"An ideologist, well, that's what he believes he is."

Death shuddered.

"Do not be mistaken, Sir. This is an ideologist we want for once," Mr Sharp said to Death.

"Oh,' Death said delighted, 'do go on then, Mr Sharp."

Toxicity

"So, have you done much in the way of politics before Mr Black?"

"Unfortunately, none that I can talk about," Death said with a wink.

"Ah, I see. I understand a thing or two about classified," Douglas said, smirking.

The plan and meeting were going well. Douglas Roach was eating out of the palm of Death's hand and to everyone's amazement, the food at the restaurant wasn't atrocious. The restaurant was more like a pub but it was quaint and clean however the lighting was horrid and everyone struggled to see what they were actually eating.

"Now you mentioned you had suggestions for my politics. Ways to make this country great again?" asked Mr Roach.

"Indeed. With the right campaign and you at the helm leading it all, this country could become one of the strongest in the world. Before the nineteen hundreds, Urit was known for tree logging and being a giant in the metal industry but since the World Wars and this nation landing on the wrong side at the end of both of them, it has fallen by the wayside."

"Yes, it is sad to lose one's position in the world. It is hard to see the way

Germany has bounced back from the wars but we have been unable to do the same. My nation is hardly ever spoken about now and we have very few countries wanting to make trade deals with us."

"So, we agree that we are of the same mind here?"

"Yes of course."

"Excellent because this is the only aspect of your politics that I wish to impose on and have an input. I'm a patriot you see."

"As am I. But tell me Mr Black, how do we make Urit great again? What is holding this country back in your opinion?"

Death smiled but to onlookers, it would have appeared more as a snarl.

"Mr Sharp, will you answer this one for me please?"

"Of course,' Mr Sharp said, leaning in and lowering his voice, 'Laskians."

"Excuse me?" said Mr Roach.

"After World War II, millions of Laskians fled their country and went to Urit. But they have not assimilated to the way of life here and the way of the Urit people. They are different to the Uritans who are the true citizens of this country. This difference they possess means they cannot be trusted. They're what's holding this country back. We must eliminate all the Laskians to restore this nation to what it once was. Give it back to its true people, the natives, the originals."

Douglas Roach looked from Mr Sharp to Death then to Anne. He was quite shocked. He took a breath.

"I'm not entirely sure how popular that view will be amongst the voters," Douglas finally said.

"Our mutual friend Professor Wick has conducted some surveys and has found that the people of Urit have very negative views on Laskians," Mr Sharp answered.

"Really? I must have missed that one," Mr Roach said surprised.

"You should read it, Mr Roach. The findings are very... intriguing," Mr Sharp.

"The general consensus the survey by Professor Wick came to is that the Uritans strongly believe the Laskians should go back to where they belong - to Laskia," Death added.

"According to the survey it is believed by many Uritans that the Laskians steal all the jobs here and have most of the wealth whilst the original people of Urit live in poverty," Anne concurred.

"It's an outrage!" Death added.

Mr Sharp gave Death a side glance as he thought Death was overdoing it a bit.

Mr Sharp continued, "This is what we're talking about Mr Roach. Millions of Laskians live here now, and the people of Urit want them gone."

"But I find it hard to believe that the people of Urit want to get rid of all the Laskians just because they are wealthy and own many businesses?" Douglas said unsure.

"Is it that hard to believe? It is the truth, after all, Mr Roach," Death said praying on Douglas' prejudice.

"Mr Roach you have much to learn about humans. One concept I think you should quickly learn is the philosophy of 'The Other'. The idea of 'The Other' is one of the strongest ideas that has ever been created," Anne said.

'The Other' wasn't exactly a philosophy- unless it is believed that racism was a philosophy rather than just pure discrimination. Anne was not being completely untruthful here though. The idea of 'The Other' was a very old idea, ancient really and is still just as prevalent today as it was thousands of years ago. The basis of the idea of 'The Other' is an individual or individuals who are viewed by a group or another individual as not belonging; that they are different in some fundamental way. More information can be obtained about this concept from philosophy or literature or just general human history. Most humans at one point have had the idea of 'The Other' at least once, on what scale the thought happens is really what matters. Death and his team were hoping the idea of 'The Other' would be on the scale of mass murder as it had worked in the past for many a leader.

Douglas Roach pondered over the idea of 'The Other' for a while. Nothing that the three people in front of him had said was in conflict with his own personal views, but he didn't want to give that away just yet. He did not like the Laskians nor did his party but for now, his views and the party's views on Laskians had been discreet. There was a low-key known opinion about the level of negativity towards the Laskians amongst the people of Urit. He knew he was not alone in his distaste for them but was there *enough* intolerance in the nation? Was this really what would win him the election? The Laskians were a minority, to be sure, and he knew that he had to play on the majority's views, this was politics after all.

"So, you really believe once all the Laskians are gone Urit will be a great nation once more?"

"Absolutely," Death replied.

"And what exactly would 'gone' be? Do we deport them all back to Laskia?"

"Deport? That is a band-aid solution. We need a more permanent solution to the Laskian problem," said Death.

"Permanent meaning what?"

"Permanent meaning terminate, Mr Roach."

Douglas's eyes widened.

"You need to think of your true people here, Mr Roach and their safety."

"And their children's children's safety," Anne quickly added.

"Urit and its people will not be safe until all the Laskians that live here are exterminated," said Death.

"Search your feelings, Mr Roach. You know it to be true," Mr Sharp concluded.

Douglas thought for a moment and then nodded. "So what would the plan be exactly?" He asked.

Death felt giddy. He turned to Mr Sharp gleefully.

"Take it away once more please, Mr Sharp," Death said.

"The elections are coming up this year, so you will need a strong campaign."

"But I'm not even in the running to become the leader of my party. There's plenty of people who are preferred over me."

"How many would you say exactly?" Anne asked.

"At least ten."

Anne looked at Death and shrugged.

"That's not a problem, Mr Roach. Leave it with us," Anne said with perfect ease.

Douglas looked at the three with slight concern.

"What's your plan for dealing with the other candidates?" He asked.

"Ignorance is bliss, Mr Roach. Besides, it's better if you focus on the campaign and we'll take care of odds and ends," Mr Sharp replied.

In consistence with his nature, Douglas left the question there and had a daydream about campaigning. Death looked over at

Anne. He could see the wheels turning in her mind. Death leaned over so he could whisper in her ear.

"I have a feeling those ten are going to become very unlucky. One or two might fall down some stairs."

"Not to mention how unsafe these roads are," she whispered.

"And those damn heart conditions they have. It's so scary; one could go any minute."

"I hear choking on food is becoming increasingly common nowadays."

Anne and Death beamed at one another. Douglas took a large gulp of his beer. Mr Sharp had kept one ear open to Anne and Death's conversation.

"Natural as always, Sir," Mr Sharp whispered in Death's ear.

"As always. Now back to the campaign," Death said.

"Once the other potentials are dealt with, we shall work on creating the perfect campaign by using propaganda. We will supply the minds of the citizens Urit with anti-Laskian thoughts. They will live and speak nothing but distaste for them."

"But, what about all the other problems in the country?"

"Well, naturally, they will all be fixed once the Laskians are dead."

"Really?"

"Of course, Mr Roach! Have you not been listening? They are the real problem. They are the source of everything that is bad in this great nation. Once they are all dead, Urit will flourish. The people know this and they are just waiting for a strong leader like yourself to rid them of this Laskian plague," Death exclaimed.

"And using propaganda will help me win the election and help rid Urit of the Laskians? Do people even use propaganda anymore?"

"Trust me when I tell you, Mr Roach, propaganda has never left. It has been used for thousands of years; we just haven't always used that term for it."

"What other term is used?"

"Well, it's quite crude, but colloquially it's called bullshit."

"Some also call it *lies* or *politics*," Mr Sharp added.

"Which are the same things anyway," Anne mumbled.

Death continued, ignoring Anne, "and with the help of social media, we have a greater chance of reaching people. We can get those influencers to help. All you need, Mr Roach is the right person to run the campaign for you."

"And who would that be?"

"Oh, we outsource that kind of thing now," Mr Sharp said.

"You don't need to concern yourself with any of this stuff Mr Roach. We will sort it all out. All you need to worry about is smiling, making speeches and being as charming as possible. Let your views flow into the minds of others," Death said.

"We really want your fantastic personality to shine and for the people of the Urit to fall in love with you and see that you're what is best for the nation and that you know the way forward," said Anne.

"Then, they will follow you anywhere," concluded Mr Sharp.

The three had worked their magic. Douglas Roach leaned back in his chair and folded his arms across his chest. He was looking smug. He seemed so pleased with himself even though he had not done a single thing yet. Anne imagined he was thinking about all the admiring fans he was going to have soon. How the other men would look up to him; how the women would fawn over him. Watching someone fall in love with themselves was an interesting site, how an arrogance would float around them like perfume.

Douglas would soon find himself believing everything the three said to him, he would in turn infect his people with these beliefs.

Anne, Death, and Mr Sharp nodded at each other. They had created their dictator. The perfect monster, their own private killing machine. No longer a man, purely just a vessel. After a few moments of basking in his wonder, Douglas stood up. He reached out his hand, Death took it. The man and Death shook hands like partners which is never how it ends but always how it begins.

"Well, I must go, Mr Black. This has been a very eventful day but I must rest as we have a lot of work to do tomorrow."

"We do."

"Mr Sharp, Anne, I'll see you tomorrow at the office."

Anne and Mr Sharp nodded at Douglas and watched him leave the pub. Death re-took his seat.

"So, who are we using for the propaganda?"

"Joseph," Death said.

"What, Stalin?" Anne asked, confused.

"No, the other one. Goebbels. Joseph Goebbels."

"The Nazi?" Anne asked.

"That's the one."

Paint it, Black

Joseph Goebbels did not invent propaganda. As learnt before, propaganda was not a modern complex. Still, the lengths Goebbels took went to were so inspiring Death preferred to think of Goebbels as the Godfather of propaganda. He was a master of Dogmatism, the key weapon in converting the masses to Nazism. Like so many other Nazis, he took his own life towards the end of World War II using poison. Naturally, Death enlisted him upon Goebbels meeting his end as Death felt a man of that skill would be useful one day.

"Are you sure the people will go for that?" Douglas Roach said, looking quite stunned.

"If you believe it, they will believe it. You do believe it don't you, Mr Roach?" Goebbels asked with a sinister look in his eyes.

"Of... of course," Douglas replied, with a slight wobble.

Douglas and Goebbels weren't exactly hitting it off. Unfortunately, Goebbels was used to the Fuhrer and Douglas was a pale imitation of him.

"I'm just going to speak to Mr Black for a moment," Goebbels said.

Death was in the corner of Douglas' office with Anne and Mr Sharp. The three were trying to work out a way to rig the election. All the other candidates in Douglas' party had met an untimely end (naturally, the mystery around the deaths of so many members of Parliament were going to be blamed on the Laskians). These events, in turn, had made Douglas the leader of the Pavian party.

"Can't we just throw away the votes or give the wrong count?" Anne asked.

"Let me contact Stalin, I think that was his main method, but I want to be sure of the particulars," Mr Sharp said, pulling his phone out and getting up.

Anne continued to fumble through some paperwork. Death saw Goebbels and his beady eyes coming towards him. Goebbels looked surlier than usual so Death knew it wouldn't be good. Goebbels took a seat in one of the mahogany chairs.

"Sir, I do not mean to doubt you, but are you sure about Mr Roach?"

"Calm yourself, Goebbels. He is merely the face of the operation; I am the brains."

"This I do not doubt," Goebbels said sternly.

Death shook his head, "Goebbels, you must help me here. I cannot do it without you. I need you to get the word out about the Laskians and to ensure our dear Mr Roach shares *all* our views. Use whatever medium you can think of. There are more ways to reach people now than there were during the Third Reich."

"True, but his conscience seems to be getting in the way."

"Well we need to get rid of that," Death said appalled by the idea of a conscience.

The two C's – conscience and chemo, were Death's true enemies. The other C he was quite undecided on. He enjoyed it very much but it was the tunnel of the living.

"You could make a film," Anne interjected.

"A film?" Death asked.

"Yes. Put together a film that looks legit but is of course, all lies. It will showcase the evilness of the Laskians and how the people of Urit suffer because of them. Then we will broadcast it. It will be on the TV, news, and social media so the masses can access it."

"What an excellent idea, Anne."

"I agree, and I know this method has worked in the past. Playing on people's fear is the best course. Fear always turns into hate, and this way, the fear will be entertaining and served with popcorn," Goebbels added.

"Tell a big enough lie and tell it frequently and it will be believed, right, Goebbels?" Death said with a wink.

"I thought Hitler said that?" Anne asked.

Goebbels grunted.

WITHIN A WEEK, GOEBBELS (with the help of Anne and Mr Sharp) had managed to film and edit a propaganda film to showcase to the people of Urit. The film was a ninety-minute masterpiece that highlighted the negative effect the Laskians were having on Urit and its *authentic* people. Goebbels was impressed with how far filmmaking had come since his day yet he still made the film in black and white for a reason that he explained to Death which Death did not understand and quickly forgot. The film or documentary was called 'The Threat of the Laskians'. It was quite a hit. Douglas was surprisingly of great help to the movie by using a slightly questionable IT company he had connections with to plaster the film all over the internet. Social media blew up with trolls hating on the Laskians and multiple twitter wars erupted. The film got people talking and thinking but mostly hating and fearing. Some people in society pointed out on social media how racist and untrue the documentary worse, but the comments were swiftly removed as were the people who wrote them.

The infamous Professor Wick showed the film in all of his lectures which helped lead to the fear of the Laskians being spread amongst the academics. Wick and Roach also showed the film to their cult. Soon the distaste for Laskians was widespread across the country. The three, Goebbels and Douglas Roach took a back seat as they watched the anarchy unfold. The damage had been done. Society would take care of the rest.

THE SMITH FAMILY WAS sitting at the table for dinner one night. Mary Smith had made everyone's favourite, her famous roast chicken with mushroom sauce.

"So, what did you learn in school today, Timmy?" Mary asked.

"Teacher had us watch a documentary."

"Oh, that had us watch that one too. About the Laskians right?" Lucy interjected.

"Why are we paying for a school to teach you about them? What about Urit history?" John Smith asked, quite outraged.

"No, it was really cool dad. The Laskians are so weird compared to us. Do you know how much better our country would be without them? They're totally holding us back," Lucy continued.

"Sweetheart, I think we should go see this film. They're playing it at the local theatre," Mary told her husband.

"I already know all these things."

"Come on, darling, if the children have seen it then we should too. We could see it for date night on Friday."

"Date night watching a film about the Laskians, oh great," John said, disgusted.

Mary smiled and shook her head.

"They've moved all the Laskian kids into separate classrooms so we don't have to be near them anymore. Apparently, they carry diseases so you shouldn't get too close to one," Lucy said.

"Oh, really. Timmy isn't your best friend George a Laskian?" Mary asked.

"Yeah," Timmy said, looking upset.

His mother patted him on the arm.

"You'll make another friend, dear."

"A non-Laskian one," his father added.

The family continued to eat their dinner. Timmy pushed his carrots around the plate as he wondered what the big deal about being Laskian was anyway.

RIOTING IN THE STREETS broke out a fortnight after the film was released. Social media and the internet were flooded with posts of the evilness of the Laskians. All the businesses the Laskians owned were looted and torn apart. A line of red paint was painted across the front door of homes Laskians resided. Slowly schools refused education to Laskian children. The current government took away any benefits they usually received. The people of Urit now viewed Laskians as non-human. They were considered lower than other animals. The violence had begun and murder would soon follow. The next step was Douglas Roach becoming President. He would be the solution to the problem of the Laskian.

The Sound of Silence

"It really is quite a coincidence all the other candidates in the party dying, leaving me as the sole leader," Douglas said as Anne fixed his tie.

"Yes, it's very fortunate for you," Mr Sharp said with a tone.

Anne rolled her eyes as Goebbels questioned his position in death. The mood in Douglas' office was not exactly high, but what would one expect with such company? Douglas Roach was preparing to give his speech to the people in hopes he could convince them to vote for him and his party... well what was left of his party. Anne dabbed a bit of powder on his face with a makeup brush.

"Now remember to be fierce but friendly," Goebbels said.

"Are they not two completely different things?" Douglas asked.

"Yes, but that is what you are. You are a friend to the people but also their enemy should they ever step out of line and doubt you."

Douglas nodded. Goebbels was not entirely convinced what had just been said was understood, but he decided to let it go.

"Speak with confidence. Don't look at the cards too much. Choose a spot at the back of the crowd and remain focused on it," Goebbels continued.

"Got it."

"Time," Mr Sharp called.

Douglas gave all of his colleagues an individual nod. Then he walked outside, standing in front of the Government House to address the people. The crowd cheered; cameras flashed. The colleagues stayed inside and watched Douglas from a high corner window in Government house. Douglas cleared his throat and began.

"To the true Citizens of Urit, I speak to you now as an equal, as one of you. I see the fear in your eyes, and I have this fear too. But why do we have this fear? What is the real name of this fear? The name is Laskian. I'm sure you have all seen the alarming, but highly factual film 'The Threat of the Laskians'. It has opened all our eyes to the evilness of these beings. The danger they are to you, to me, to our children. I urge you to vote true. I urge you to vote for the Pavion party. Only we can end the tyranny of the Laskians. Only we can make this country safe again."

Douglas paused. The mob cheered and clapped. Douglas felt more at ease. He continued.

"Should I and my party be given the honour of serving this great nation, we would exterminate the threat of the Laskian. However, we admit we would need help in this endeavour. The party will need the full support of the people."

"You have it, Douglas," a member of the crowd yelled out.

"We stand with you," another screamed.

"Exterminate the Laskians," many bellowed.

"My people, your words give me strength. You are strong. We are strong. Our only weakness is them, and you know of whom I speak of."

"The vicious Laskians," a crowd member called.

"They're the problem! They are why our country is failing," another yelled.

"Yes, my brother. And how will we exterminate this threat? How will we rid ourselves of these vermin? How do we make this country great again?"

"Kill all the Laskians," a boy of ten called out.

"YES!" The crowd yelled in unison.

"Yes, my people! Take out your weapons. No harm shall come to you from myself or my government. Harm will only come from the Laskians. We will not be safe until every last Laskian is dead. Kill them, kill them all!"

The scene that followed this speech reminded Death of the storming of the Bastille. The crowd scattered like cockroaches. They ran into their houses and came back out with guns and axes. Doors with the red slash of the mark of a Laskian were smashed in, and the homes raided. All that could be heard in the streets of Urit were gunshots, screams and cheers. What could be seen was something else. Women were being dragged out by their hair, men were being beaten before welcoming a bullet to free them of their pain and fear. Laskian children looked on in terror as their parents were murdered right before their eyes. The grey walls and streets turned to red.

Of course, not all Uritans joined in on the violence. Many thought how horrible it was. Some even cried at the sight of the bloodshed. But not one, not one intervened, not one defended a Laskian. Most stood in silence, grateful that it wasn't happening to them, relieved they were not Laskian.

LITTLE TIMMY SMITH watched the brutality from his bedroom window. His mother was outside holding a Laskian woman's hair up and chopping it off with scissors. He could see his father beating a man. His sister was spitting on the Laskian bodies that lay on the ground. Timmy looked down at the action figure he held in his hand that George the Laskian gave him for his birthday last year. He hoped his friend was okay.

DEATH FELT HIS PHONE ring in his pocket. He pulled it out and answered it.

"Mr D?"

"Yes, Aurora?"

"The numbers are skyrocketing. Has it begun?"

"Yes, yes it has."

Death hung up, but then his phone made a noise again. It was a text from his wife. The text was the emoji of a skull followed by a winky face blowing a kiss.

My First My Last My Everything

Death was out walking the streets of Uni Ted, a daily occurrence for him now as he loved the carnage. The massacre of the Laskians had left red stains all over the streets and buildings. Urit had found its new colour. Within a month, one million Laskians had been slaughtered. The government had dug a massive hole in the forest with earth movers as a place to bury all the bodies. Any Laskians that were left had either gone into hiding or attempted to flee into neighbouring countries, only to be met at the border with a bullet to the head. The rest of the world had not heard of the slaughtering that was happening in Urit as the police of Urit were now resembling the KGB. However, there were whispers brewing. The world was a different place now than when other genocides happened. Modern media was a friend and foe to information. The events that had happened in Urit could not be contained for long. There were always a few morally righteous individuals who would ruin it for everyone else.

Death decided to take a look at the grave where all the dead Laskians had been dropped into. The grave was situated deep in the forest and the smell of pine filled Death's nose. After the killings, the army loaded the bodies into trucks and went into the forest to clear room for a massive hole. The dead Laskian bodies were poured into the pit like cement. Death took in the beauty of the grave; he had seen countless graves and cremations in his time but could never get enough. Something caught Death's eye as he marvelled at the grave. There was a small action figure sitting on the left side corner of the grave. Death looked around the forest but could see no one. He bent down and picked up the figurine. He felt such a sense of innocence and sadness attached to it. Death swiftly put the toy back down. Despair he could swallow, but innocence was always somewhat bitter to him. Death decided to continue on with his walk.

Death eventually arrived at Government House. He needed to have a very frank conversation with Douglas if the plan was to go further. Government House had received a makeover once Douglas took power. The seventies décor of the building had been replaced with a clinical feel. The walls were now white, the furniture was white, the lights were white, and the carpet (in true Urit style) was grey. One would suppose it was an improvement but they feel of the building resembled a cancer ward which made Death feel right at home but everyone else felt an uneasiness they could not explain.

The election had really just been a formality after Douglas' speech and the killing begun. In turn, the colleagues did not need to rig the election. Douglas won by a landslide. His party had complete control of the government. There were a few opposing government figures but they had very little power and posed no real threat for now. Douglas was relishing in his role as President. He was adored by all (except for the Laskians but who counted them). He had a different woman every night, only drank the finest champagne and had become a slave to consumerism. Mr Sharp had to keep an eye on his spending so the country didn't go broke.

When Death walked into Douglas' office he found him in a compromising but pleasurable state. Douglas was in his leather chair, arms behind his head and he was grinning. Death could see the black high heel shoes with a red sole poking out from under the desk. When Douglas noticed Death he was very startled and quite embarrassed.

"Mr...Mr Black... I'm so sorry" he stammered.

Death put his hand up.

"Calm yourself Douglas, I'll come back in a couple of minutes."

Death walked outside and sat in a white fur chair whilst Douglas and the woman finished. As Death waited he received a text from his wife.

Have you told him yet? xo

Just about too xx

A couple of minutes later a very pretty blonde left Douglas' office. Death re-entered and took a seat across from Douglas. Douglas had kept his mahogany furniture – it made him feel more regal than the white.

"I must again apologise, Mr Black."

"Don't worry about it, Douglas. A man like you should never apologise."

"Thank you, Mr Black. So what do I owe this honour for? Was there something on your mind?"

"There is Douglas. I feel we have reached that point in the relationship where trust is what will bind us and lack of it will break us."

"Okay," Douglas said, unsure.

"You see, I have not been fully honest with you, Douglas."

"You haven't?"

"Well, with most things I have been, but I cannot lie to you anymore, I respect and care for you far too much. And it is not smart to conceal things from a man such as yourself."

Douglas' ego was on steroids now.

"I would not think it wise either."

Well, well, look who had grown a pair, Death thought.

"So, what truth must you reveal?"

"I must reveal who I am, Douglas."

Douglas was silent. He looked Death up and down.

"Well, who are you, Mr Black?"

"You see, that's just it, Douglas. I'm not Mr Black."

"Oh?"

"Give it a thought, Douglas. You're an intelligent man. I'm sure you can work it out... no matter how farfetched it may seem..."

Douglas leant back in his chair. If he was honest, he really didn't know anything about Mr Black even still. Douglas had needed Mr Black for money, backing and connections; the rest was immaterial. Politicians were taught early on never to ask too many questions. He was sure though, that his name wasn't Mr Black, as he often heard Anne call him Mr D. Apart from that the few characteristics he had observed were his taste in expensive suits, his old way of speaking and his complete obsession with Death.

Death could see the wheels turning in Douglas' mind, but the lightbulb moment did not seem to be happening.

"Well, let's start with my name Douglas as a name seems to be very important to your kind. I do not have a normal name like you; it's more a title. I have more than one name that I have been called but the most common in the English language starts with D."

There was only one word that came to Douglas' mind.

"Death?"

Death nodded, baring his teeth in the widest of smiles.

"But..."

Douglas was stunned. He had so many questions overtaking his mind. This could not be possible. He knew about the Grim Reaper, but the man or rather the being in front of him, was not how he imagined. Death did not wear tailored suits, have colleagues, eat, or have a sense of humour. Douglas felt his chest constricting. This could not be. Maybe Douglas himself was dead and he didn't know it, was this all a dream? Was this the afterlife?

Death saw the terror that was engulfing Douglas. He got up and walked over to him. He put his hand gently on Douglas' shoulder.

"Calm yourself, my friend. I am not here for you. I want you alive."

"You do?"

"Of course, Douglas. You are my prodigy. Think of me as just a simple businessman and you as my partner."

Douglas' breath returned to him which he hoped was a clear indication that he was still living. He looked over the being that stood before him.

"You're not exactly what I... imagined."

"Ah, yes, well if you are referring to a scythe and black hooded cloak, this is merely myth. I have never had such things. Naturally, I have changed my look over the years but I have always looked like one of the humans so I could be among you, and fit in if you would."

Death sat back down in his seat.

"So, all this... everything that has happened in Urit was just to help you and the... business as you call it?"

"I must admit Douglas, that part of this has been about helping me and the business, but only partly. I looked at your magnificent country and took pity on it for I saw the potential if only a few were expelled from it. The Laskians, in my view, truly are rodents that must be expelled from the earth. You know why I do not like the Laskians Douglas?"

Douglas shook his head.

"They are different to every other human."

"Well, I know this."

"No, Douglas, I mean their DNA is not like the rest. They're mutants. They carry odd components in their blood that I have never seen in any other human."

"I knew it!' Douglas said, nodding furiously, 'we must eradicate their kind or all humans will suffer."

It was amazing how hate could mask most things. A complete falsehood about the Laskians having different DNA to other humans was more shocking to Douglas Roach than the Grim Reaper sitting before him. Death decided to continue with the façade.

"No one else could do all this but you, Douglas."

"Was I your only choice?"

"Of course, Douglas, how could you doubt it?"

Douglas did not doubt it. A true tyrant must be narcissistic if you are going to get anywhere with him.

"So, we will continue our partnership?"

"There's no one I would rather be partnered with, Douglas."

"I will not let you down, Sir. You have given Urit and me so much, I only hope I can repay your kindness and be useful to you."

The two men stood up. Douglas walked over to Death and shook his hand.

"Please, Douglas, call me Mr D."

Carry on Wayward Son

"**I** think it's time to expand, Mr D. We must take our mission to the next phase," Douglas said excitedly.

Death was in Douglas' office mulling over a report Mr Sharp had just given him. Death was grinning as he was very pleased with the headway that had been made. Laskians were almost extinct in the Urit. The numbers coming through to headquarters were astonishing.

"Did you hear me, Mr D?" Douglas asked.

"Oh, sorry Douglas, I was just admiring our progress. What were you saying?"

Douglas got up from behind the desk and walked around to face Death on the couch. He leaned against the desk and folded his arms. He stared down at Death and looked very serious.

"I want to invade the homeland of the Laskians. I want to invade Laskia. Urit and the world will not truly be safe until every Laskian is exterminated."

Death stopped gawking at the report; this was even better. Douglas Roach now had a vision, Death's vision. Death liked this idea very much.

"Well, the surest way to get away with mass murder is to cover it up with something else."

"I completely agree."

"Well then, Douglas, let's go to war."

"WE'RE GOING TO INVADE Laskia?" Mr Sharp asked.

"Yes, isn't it brilliant? It was Douglas' idea and I do believe it's about time we took this operation to the next level."

"Do you think we can, though?" Anne asked, hesitantly.

"Of course! We can and we must. We've killed all the Laskians in Urit anyway. It's time for expansion. And I figure once we have wiped out this group of people, we can start on our next victims."

"But Sir, won't the other countries interject?" asked Mr Sharp.

"I doubt it. The Laskians are not exactly the most popular of people anywhere in the world. Also, I asked Goebbels to develop messages of propaganda all over the world in anticipation."

"Oh, which one did he use?" Asked Anne.

"The usual, the one we used for Urit – Laskians have all the money, they are different from the rest of us, they're stealing all the jobs etc."

"Oh nice, the original ones, they never fail. I suppose the main countries won't join initially, as they have other threats to deal with now?"

"Exactly and I can think of a few nations that just downright don't and won't care."

"Are you sure the main countries won't butt in?" Anne asked.

"Oh, they won't join bother. Laskia and Urit are not prevalent enough in the world to make the big nations abandon their own lands and people."

"And the rest?"

"They might impose some sanctions but they will have little impact on Urit. Urit is such a loner of a country and so minimal that it hardly deals with other nations."

Anne and Mr Sharp nodded.

"So, what's our next step?" Anne asked.

"We put it to the Government."

THE VOTE TO INVADE Laskia was unanimously for. Well technically, there were a few members of the government who opposed the notion but Death and his colleagues knew how to take care of them.

"Douglas, have you ever read much about Stalin and the USSR? I think brushing up on your knowledge about that time would be very beneficial," Death suggested.

Douglas and the three had gotten wind of a private dinner that all of the opposing (and dismally remaining) Government figures were going to. They were planning a coup to not only stop the invasion of Laskia but also to overthrow Douglas and his party. Douglas acquired this information from one of the Government figures' mistresses that gave the information to Douglas in hopes of becoming his mistress and leaving the overweight, balding idiot that was the Secretary of Trade. Anne and Mr Sharp found the chef who was making the meals for the Government figures. They bribed him with one million pounds to poison the dinner. Douglas's remaining opposition died within twenty-four hours (another win for Death). Douglas had absolute power now. Everything was in place for the invasion of Laskia.

"Okay, it has been confirmed by the doctors. All the opposing figures of the government are dead," Anne said, walking into Douglas' office beaming.

"Excellent! Well done, Douglas. We should celebrate," Death said.

"I agree, Mr D. Let me get the champagne."

By 'me', Douglas meant his assistant, who walked in with a bottle of Champagne and four flutes.

"Cheers," the four said as they clinked their glasses together.

"Thank you, Mr D and thank you for suggesting that I brush up on my Cold War history. The USSR and Stalin are so inspiring. I might do most things the 'Stalin way' from now," Douglas said.

"Except for when it comes to comedy. Use British influence for that."

"Oh yeah, good point,' Douglas said, taking a mouthful of Champagne, 'is it time now then, Mr D? Do you think we are ready? My army is awaiting orders."

"Yes it, Douglas. Let the next level begin!"

"HERE'S YOUR SPEECH, Mr Roach," Mr Sharp said, handing Douglas a piece of paper.

It was now time for Douglas to give possibly the most important speech of his career. He was about to tell his people, the Laskians, the world, that he... as in Urit... would be invading Laskia.

"Thank you, Mr Sharp,' Douglas said as he skimmed over the piece of paper, 'any changes made?"

"Minimal."

"Great."

The three colleagues and Douglas were backstage at the Regal Theatre. The crowd were cheering in anticipation of the curtains being lifted and Douglas emerging. Douglas kept adjusting his stance and staring at his feet.

"You will be great, Douglas," Death assured him.

"I am a bit nervous."

"Don't be. They cannot wait to see you. Listen."

Douglas stood still and lifted his gaze to the ceiling. The crowd was saying one thing – his name. Confidence overtook Douglas. His transition from mediocre to sublime was complete.

Anne did a quick last-minute fix of Douglas' tie and fluffed his hair up a bit.

"I think we're ready," she said.

Douglas looked at three colleagues and gave them a nervous smile.

"Well, here it goes."

Finally the red curtains were lifted. Douglas stepped out onto the stage. Cheers turned to silence. Not a sound could be heard apart from Douglas's shoes as he walked across the stage towards the microphone. The moment Douglas was in front of the microphone and stationary he lifted his arms up in the form of a V. The crowd erupted. Everyone in the theatre were cheering and clapping. Anne, Mr Sharp and Death watched on from the side lines. All three marvelled at the sight before them. They were all beaming as they were incredibly proud of what and whom had been created. But Death wondered if it was himself, Anne and Mr Sharp that had truly created Douglas Roach – the man, the myth, the monster? He was only just a man but had fable and prejudice really made him into the God-like creature the mob saw him as? Or was that it, was it really the mob's doing? Death was feeling quite inadequate and unnecessary now. Who was the real creator here?

After quite a few minutes of pure vanity Douglas dropped his arms and the crowd became silent. The lights shone on Douglas. He looked at the pages in front of him. With an unwavering sense of righteousness, Douglas spoke.

"To the true citizens of this nation, I address you now. Our strength is our quickness and our brutality. Genghis Khan had thousands of people hunted down and killed, deliberately and with a gay heart, but we have already done better than thousands. We have slaughtered millions. History sees in him a great ruler. What this weak and pathetic world alleges about me does not matter. I have given the order and will have everyone shot who utters but one word of criticism against myself, my party, or the greatness of this nation. The aim of this war does not consist in reaching certain designated geographical lines, but in the enemies' physical elimination. Thus I put forward the order to kill without pity or mercy all men, women, and children of the Laskian race or language. Only thus will we gain the living space that we need. For whom still talks nowadays of the extermination of past races and religions?"

There was a pause as the crowd took in the words of Douglas Roach. Then they chanted, it was nothing very profound, just as before, it was purely his name. They said his name over and over again with a fist pump to go with it. Douglas loved every minute of his glory. He stood on the stage waving and smiling. They loved him and he loved them.

"I feel as if I have heard this speech before or a version of it at least," Death said to Anne and Mr Sharp.

"You have, Sir," Mr Sharp replied.

"Really? When?"
"1939, but it would have been said in German then."

Brilliant Disguise

"Oh, Mr D, thanks so much for coming to see me."

"Not a problem, Douglas," Death said as he walked into Douglas' office.

Douglas was in the middle of packing up his office before the invasion of Laskia. Mr Sharp had explained to Douglas Roach that it was uncommon for a President to lead an invasion but Douglas insisted. Douglas wanted to lead his army into Laskia and have the glory and praise for doing such a daring act himself. Of course, Douglas would not be doing any of the actual fighting, but the picture of him putting his foot on Laskian soil would be great for publicity.

"Please take a seat," Douglas said, gesturing to the leather couch.

The couch was covered in paperwork. Death pushed it aside and sat down. Douglas dragged his chair over and sat across from Death.

"How goes the invasion plan, Douglas?"

"Very well. We expect to land this time next week. The army is ready and willing. The Laskians will be so surprised."

"Yes indeed."

There was silence. Death looked around the room as he waited for Douglas to get to the real point of the meeting.

"Mr D... may I ask you a few questions?" He said, lowering his voice and leaning forward.

"Of course."

Death knew this conversation would happen eventually. Not many mortals can meet Death and have no questions for him. Mortals pondered over Death nearly as much as they did about life.

"It's about you and your ah... line of work."

"I understand. Feel free to ask what you wish, Douglas. You and I have no secrets."

Douglas smiled. This was almost becoming boring for Death; Douglas made it so easy.

"I should just start by saying I mean no disrespect in my questions. I'm just inquisitive."

"As you should be."

Douglas nodded. He looked nervous.

"How old are you, Mr D?"

"Old. Ancient, really."

"But, when did you come into... being?"

"There's no specific year for that as it was a time pre-human but think of my death span as whenever there was life, in any form, there was me."

"And Anne and Mr Sharp?"

"Anne came to work for me during the Black Death, and Mr Sharp well... him I have known for thousands of years."

"Really?"

"Oh yes. Mr Sharp was my first employee."

"Could I be considered for employment afterlife?"

No.

"Yes, of course, Douglas, but let's focus on what you can do in life now for the moment."

"Oh yes, of course."

"Do you have a home?"

"Of course, Douglas. I live in the eastern part of the continent. I even have a wife and three dogs."

Douglas smiled.

"Are your headquarters there?"

"They are."

There was another awkward pause.

"Was there anything else, Douglas?"

"Well, your work Mr D, your business..."

"Yes?"

"You enjoy it?"

"Oh very much. I take my work very seriously and over the past few decades, my losses have been really low."

"Which is bad?" Douglas asked, confused.

"In my line of work losses are profits. The more the better."

"Ah, yes I see," Douglas said nodding.

"I've been doing this job since the dawn of life, I love it and like any businessman, I want my business to succeed otherwise I feel like a failure. We all want to be successful in what we do."

"I completely agree."

"And with your help, Douglas you have made my business successful again."

"Right..."

"And you have made your country and the world a safer and better place," Death added quickly.

"Well, that has been my aim, Mr D. I'm just trying to make my country and the world a restored place for future generations. It's really all for the children."

"Yes, of course, the children," Death said, nodding.

The ideas Douglas had convinced himself and his people of were baffling. Douglas truly believed the garbage he was emitting. Death thought the whole process would be more complex. The plan he and the colleagues had thought was too simple, too vintage, yet somehow, it was working. Death feared at the beginning of the project; humans were not so easily swayed these days. He was happily proved wrong. Humans were still just as effortlessly manipulated. Their hatred towards one another and the determination to find differences instead of similarities was just as compelling as ever. Douglas truly and honestly believed he was doing some great work. For the first time in a long time, Death's concerns about his business eased off. Life could not prosper here.

"I think we should conclude our conversation there for the moment."

"Are you sure, Douglas? Don't you want to know what it's like *after...*" Death said, menacingly.

Douglas hesitated.

"No... I'm sure. I'm intrigued to know more but also a bit scared to as well. It's usually such an unknown, but now that I finally have the horse's mouth in the room... I find myself hesitating."

"It's a bit like a magician's trick."

"I'm sorry?"

"You want to know how the magician does it, but when you find out the answer, it's usually anticlimactic, and you wish you were still ignorant."

Douglas leaned back in his chair and nodded.

"You're right, Mr D. Ignorance is bliss."

"That it is, Douglas. That it is."

"Well, at least I know I have a friendly face to find when I meet my end."

Death laughed and nodded. He knew Douglas was going straight to the afterlife. He would not stop at go and collect two hundred dollars. He would see no one and be no one in death. A person who was easily manipulated in life would be of no use in death.

"Well, this was a great chat, Douglas. I feel we are even closer," Death said, getting up.

"I do too, Mr D."

Douglas stood up and shook Death's hand. Death nodded and smiled and left the office. Death walked outside of Government House onto the main road. The street was bumper to bumper with army tanks and military personnel. They were on their way to Laskia and what they thought was glory. The soldiers marched with their chests puffed out. Their pride for their nation and the cause was seeping from them. It was not a unique sight. Death had seen it many times before. How crisp the uniforms looked, how strong and tall the men marched, how fresh and clean the guns were. Death ducked into one of the cafés. He ordered a latte, sat by the window, and watched the parade. Death could kick back now; the humans were doing the work for him. He sipped his coffee and listened to the soldiers sing their marching song.

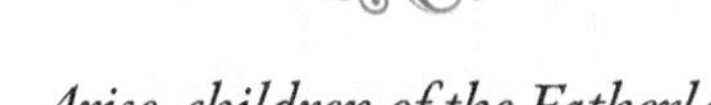

Arise, children of the Fatherland
Our day of glory has arrived
Against us the bloody flag of tyranny
is raised; the bloody flag is raised.
Do you hear, in the countryside

The roar of those ferocious soldiers?
They're coming right into your arms
To cut the throats of your sons, your comrades!
To arms, citizens!
Form your battalions
Let's march, let's march
That their impure blood
Should water our fields.

Hello.... (the Adele version)

"Sir, have you looked at the death toll right now?" Mr Sharp asked.

"I have indeed, Mr Sharp, and I are very happy," Death replied, staring at the television.

Mr Sharp followed Death's line of sight. He was staring at the TV in the corner of the bunker where a journalist was on screen reporting on the situation in Laskia. They showed footage of bombed buildings, homes, women, men, and children.. Laskia was being raised to the ground. Rubble covered the city with limbs and intestines scattered throughout. It was chaos. It was ugly. It was absolutely delicious.

Douglas and the Uritan army had invaded Laskia nearly four months ago. It was an easy invasion, but many are. Laskia and its people were completely blindsided. They had no idea that genocide was being committed against its people in Urit. They had heard a few whispers and rumours, but the Laskias never thought there was any truth to them. To make matters worse for them, the surrounding countries of Urit claimed they had no idea of the atrocities being committed just next door to them. The main problem for Laskia was its lack of military personnel, weapons, and general defence. The soldiers of Urit immensely outnumbered the soldiers of Laskia. After the speech, Douglas was overwhelmed by the support he received from his people. Women and children were even signing up to join the war effort.

Once the initial invasion had occurred, Laskia asked for help from its neighbouring countries, if truth be told it asked for help from most nations. To no great surprise, no one could answer the call and what Death had predicted become a reality. Many of the countries felt they should not be involved in this conflict; it was not their war to fight. Other nations simply did not like the Laskians or care about them enough to risk their own people. Some sanctions (as expected) were put in place but sanctions do not halt an assault. The armed forces of Urit had suffered very few losses during the invasion and since (which was quite vexing for Death but it kept Douglas happy). A rumour from an unknown source was whispered about things becoming nuclear should anyone try to interfere with Urit and its invasion. A threat Death hoped would be made real. How Urit had supposedly acquired these nuclear weapons, no one knew. The country did not possess them before the invasion and perhaps it was all a lie but no one was game enough to take the risk. Douglas and his army had won before they even arrived.

Death and his colleagues had set themselves up in a bunker the Laskians built for themselves. The Uritan army found this bunker on day five of the invasion. Two hundred Laskians were crammed inside. They were all forced out and shot, well after they had dug their own mass grave that is. The bunker was dark with only dimly lit lamps for light. It was set under a hill and there was a constant sound of dripping water. Death had exclusive rights to the bunker by order of Douglas who came and went from it. They had been set up with four desks, chairs, laptops, and a fridge. Mr Sharp seemed quite at ease in this environment but Anne was struggling somewhat.

"Anne, are you watching this?" Death called out as he looked around the bunker for her.

"You know I'm not."

Anne was planning away at one of the desks.

"Still angry with me, Anne?"

"Of course I am."

Death went over to Anne and sat next to her. She didn't look up but continued to handwrite the next battle plan.

"Anne, listen to me. It's common knowledge that all great dictators must have a bunker. They need somewhere to plan and live while a war is going on."

"I hate being in here. It's so stuffy."

"Well, you're not exactly in need of air, Anne."

Anne pouted.

"But... I... bunkers often get bombed, and people die in them."

"Which will affect you how?"

Anne looked up at Death and scowled at him. That joke would always be too soon for Anne. She turned away from Death and went back to writing. He took the pen off her and held her hand.

"It's not forever."

"But death is."

There was silence between the two. Death dropped her hand. Tears were forming in her eyes. The calm blueness of them was turning into a storm. This often happened to Anne; less and less as the centuries went by but her emotions would always flare up when things in the world were particularly bad. Her grief and pain would consume her and she would try to hurt everyone around her, which was usually Death or Mr Sharp.

"We should go for a walk?"

Anne raised her eyebrows.

"Where? In one of the lovely parks Douglas and his army just blew up?"

A CASUAL WALK AMID a war zone is an interesting one that very few ever experience.

"This is hideous," Anne said, watching her feet.

"This is human."

Anne stopped and turned to Death. Death could feel her anger and hurt.

"Are you sure? Because it looks a lot like you."

"I am you, Anne. I'm a part of all of you, but I have *never* forced one human to kill another. You lot do not need my help there."

Anne opened her mouth to argue, but she knew he was right. She sighed, and Death did too.

"We're not all a total loss."

"Of course not. I know that. What you did for your sister was one of the most beautiful things I have ever seen. It was so rare, so pure."

That was it for Anne; she had reached her limit. Her inner strength crumbled, as did she as she dropped to her knees. She buried her face in her hands and let the tears and emotions flow.

"I'm so useless. I couldn't save her."

Death, too, went down to his knees. He reached out his arms and pulled her towards him. He cradled her as a father would for a daughter.

"You, at that moment, where you sacrificed your life for hers, you were one of the bravest and kindest souls I had ever seen. So many people say they would sacrifice themselves for another but rarely do. Never doubt your sincerity, Anne. I know I never will."

Anne looked up at Death. She looked like a child.

"It's been hundreds of years and I still miss her. It still hurts just as much."

"You will never not miss her, Anne. That is love as I understand. True, unconditional love."

Anne moved out of Death's arms and sat on the ground. She looked defeated and tired. Anne preferred Death when he was like this. She felt a warmness to his usual disdain. In truth, she never had someone respect her as much as Death did, but she was often filled with shame when she thought about what her death had eventuated to. She was often conflicted as she felt more alive now than she did when she was with the living.

"I'm sorry. I always blame you and act distant at times."

Death shrugged, "I'm used to it."

And he was used to it, he truly was. Very few humans (and only at pivotal moments) were ever genuinely grateful to meet Death. Humans throughout history consistently failed to realise that he was necessary. Life would not be precious without Death. Not to mention how much worse overpopulation would be without him. As 'Queen' once said, who wants to live forever anyway?

"I promise you, Anne. As I always say; I'm never personal or ageist. Never racist or sexist. How many aspects of this earth do you know that can say that?"

Anne let out a little smile.

"You and cancer."

Death laughed. She had a point.

"And perhaps love."

"Love?" Death asked, taken a back.

Anne could hear the concern in Death's voice. It was almost panic.

"Yes, love. I'm sorry to break this to you Mr D but love is even stronger than you."

"I don't think so," Death said defensively.

"Even after death, after you, love goes on. Death, that is you, cannot stop it. Take my love for my sister. True there is near seven hundred years of death, but there is also seven hundred years of love."

Death felt his eye twitching. Cancer he viewed as an ally; love was an enemy. Death did not really understand love. Sure, he has a wife whom he cares about. He was also incredibly fond of Anne and enjoyed the company of many of his workers. Death loved his work though. That was is first and true love and it never wavered.

Looking off into the distance, Death said, "there's never been a plague or a war that has been able to kill love, has there? Mother Nature and I have no power there, do we?"

Anne shook her head, "it can die in a way; it can cease just like life. But it also has the power to come back and live on. Love is like you Mr D. Not exactly alive, not exactly physical but at the same time, it's everywhere."

Death got up and held out his hand to her. She took it, and he pulled her up so she was back on her feet. They looked into each other's eyes. Death placed a hand on Anne's cheek. They could both feel something, Death could even see it in Anne's eyes and her in his. The human feelings were catching more then he cared to admit.

"Don't tell me after seven centuries you have gotten wise."

"Well, I didn't want to rush it," Anne said, with a wink.

Death shook his head and smiled. They both dusted off the sand on their clothes.

"Back to it then? For I'm sure you know death never sleeps."

"You sleep all the time."

Death narrowed his eyes in annoyance, "well, I didn't mean it so literally, did I?"

Anne shook her head and smiled. The two colleagues started walking, but Anne quickly stopped.

"You know, this business of yours doesn't always come easy to me. I'm still learning."

"I can't work out of that's very human of you or very un-human of you," Death said, grinning.

Anne laughed.

"I would say... both."

"I'm sure if I had a conscience, Anne, it would look like you," Death said with a wink.

"Aren't you lucky to have such an attractive conscience, then?"

Death put his arm around Anne.

"I am the luckiest man dead."

Anne screwed up her nose, "that's not the saying."

"It is for me."

Zombie

"So, should I mention now that I'm a touch claustrophobic? This will really flare up my anxiety," Anne said, looking nervous.

"Anne, you're dead. I don't believe you can still suffer from anxiety," Death replied.

"Trust me, I can! There is no escaping anxiety," Anne said, quite offended.

"You will feel better once we're moving," Mr Sharp replied, trying to portray empathy.

"So, does that mean I'll still have an intense fear of spiders even after I die?" Douglas asked, quite concerned.

"Depends. If you are Hitler's dog dead, no. If you are Elvis dead, yes," Death answered.

Douglas nodded as if he understood Death's answer, but the three colleagues knew he was none the wiser.

"Start her up, Douglas," Death said.

"Yes, Sir," Douglas said, enthusiastically saluting Death.

Douglas was taking the team on a sightseeing tour of the work that had been accomplished in Laskia. They were using one of the army's tanks to get around in as it was deemed bullet proof and they had to be careful with Douglas.

"Now, if you will all turn to your right, you'll see a school that was bombed last week. We average about two hundred students were killed here."

"Excellent work, Douglas," Death concurred.

Mr Sharp took out his phone and started taking pictures – he liked documenting their progress. And it could be useful for historical value one day.

"Thank you, Mr D. Now, on your left you will see a place of worship for the Laskians. Naturally, we bombed all the places of worship first because we don't just want to exterminate the Laskians, we want to rid the world of their religion and all traces of them."

"Were there many Laskians hiding in the temples?"

"Thousands. Every temple was crammed to the roof with Laskians. I think the Laskians believed that places of worship would somehow protect them."

"I'm assuming it didn't," Anne mumbled.

"Now, now, Anne, none of the attitude, please. Douglas has done some incredible work here and his plan of attack has been on point," said Death.

"Next, we plan to perform an assault on the museums and any place that is culturally and historically accurate."

"Excellent. Destroy their culture and you will destroy the people. Just ensure there are people inside these buildings when you blow them up. We should try to be as economical as possible."

"Did you also eliminate the doctors and academics Mr Roach?"

"Yes, Mr Sharp, they were killed off first."

"Very good," Mr Sharp said, nodding.

"I do hope that the numbers have been to your liking so far Mr D?"

"Yes, I am very pleased."

"I'm glad to hear it. I hope I am living up to your expectation of me?"

"You are even more than I expected, Douglas, have no doubt there."

If he could, Death would have vomited up his lunch. The adoration complex that Anne and Mr Sharp had suggested had genuinely worked, but Death was beginning to tire of the constant compliments and reassurance he had to give Douglas. It felt as if Death was selling his own soul which was terribly vexing to Death as he preferred to be the buyer. On the other hand, Douglas seemed willing to do anything for Death and believe anything he said.

Unknown to Douglas, Death and his colleagues secretly found a way to have Douglas and the people in Urit turn on each other. Mr Sharp had already begun by making up a story about Douglas' generals and other notable army figures wanting to overthrow him. Douglas had them all killed for treason. He was becoming quite paranoid and murdered anyone he felt could betray him. The new plan was once all the Laskians were dead, the three colleagues would have the people of Urit turn on one another. Fear and whispers would be vital to the success of the plan. Who was a true Uritan and who was an imposter would drive the citizens of Urit. Who was loyal to the Government and who was seeking outside help would be all the new-found Government would care about. Mr Sharp and Death had delved into history once more to consolidate this plan which had been done before. Still, Death felt he could not be blamed for being the only one to learn from human history.

As Death marvelled in his cleverness, Douglas halted the tank.

"I want to show you all this particular spot," Douglas said.

The three colleagues nodded and then very ungracefully climbed out of the tank. Laskia was a desert country, and it was pretty windy today, which caused the sand to whip up into the air and land on everyone's face. Anne and Mr Sharp were somewhat protected with their glasses but Death found himself cursing sand and Mother Nature once more.

The sound of bombing and shattering buildings could be heard all around them. Death took it all in. He felt the fear, smelt the blood, heard the cries, and saw the rubble. This was a wet dream for Death. He had not felt like this since Vietnam. He could feel the tears of glee welling up in his eyes. They really had done it.

"Are you okay, Mr D?" Douglas asked.

"Oh, yes, Douglas. I'm quite at a loss for words. I am just so happy and proud of you. I don't know how to express to you my gratitude," he said, patting his eyes.

Douglas almost blushed.

"Thank you, Mr D. I so wanted to make you proud. These past months have meant so much to me and completely opened my eyes. I always wish to serve you."

"And so you shall, Douglas, so you shall."

Death looked over at Mr Sharp and Anne. Anne was pretending to fake vomit over the scene Douglas and Death were making. Mr Sharp just folded his arms across his chest and nodded, which was all the emotion one would get from him. Douglas kept looking at Death. He seemed almost jittery now.

"The death tally is the most important thing to you, Mr D?"

"Of course, Douglas. It's my reason for existence."

Douglas looked at the ground.

"I wish to serve you in the best way I can, Mr D. I want to make you proud. I must be the thing that makes you happiest."

"You have, and you are Douglas."

In his head, Death apologised to his wife for this farce.

"Thank you, Mr D, but I think there is only one way I can really make you happy. The most significant way I can make a key contribution to you and the cause. I know who you are, and what matters most is your business."

Death nodded; he wasn't sure where Douglas was going with this.

"I care about my people and my country but the Laskians are practically instinct now. I have protected the present and future generations from their threat and this was only possible because of you."

"Douglas, you flatter."

"This is the only way I can think of to show my gratitude."

Death looked at Douglas confused. He hoped Douglas wasn't about to offer him sexual favours. He was thinking to himself that he needed to reiterate that he was married before things took an interesting but uninvited turn.

"Thank you so much for everything, Mr D. This is my final act, and it's all for you. I'm sure I will see you again see though..."

Douglas' next actions appeared to have happened in slow motion. Without ever leaving Death's eyes, Douglas pulled out a handgun from his pant pocket and rested the gun against his temple. Death yelled out 'no' and lunged at Douglas. Anne and Mr Sharp could do nothing but watch. Douglas smiled and pulled the trigger.

Another One Bites the Dust

Death stared down at Douglas Roach in complete shock. Douglas had fallen to the ground the moment the bullet made impact. The blood trickled out of his head, onto the sand which quickly absorbed the red liquid. Death turned his eyes to Anne and Mr Sharp who appeared just as stunned as he was. He didn't want to believe what he had just witnessed. There was so much more to do. So much more they could have done. Anger and disappointment filled Death.

"Oh, for fuck sake!" Death finally yelled to no one.

Anne and Mr Sharp walked over to the body to further inspect the situation.

"My, that's a sight," Anne said, turning her nose up at Douglas.

Mr Sharp looked at Douglas and then back to his colleagues as he tried to find the words for such a situation.

"Well...I suppose it was out of love and complete admiration and respect for you, Sir. He truly believed in your plight and wanted to help. He gave you the ultimate gift. Another soul for you and the business," Mr Sharp said.

"That may be true, Mr Sharp, but the plan is completely ruined now!"

"Maybe we can get everyone to follow the Vice President?" Anne asked.

"I doubt it. Douglas Roach was the be-all and end-all. A true dictator. No one will follow a second-rate version; it would be like Germany after Hitler died."

"What do you want to do now then, Sir?" Mr Sharp asked.

NATURALLY, THE THREE colleagues took the only option they saw – they went back home with their tails between their legs. The moment the three of them landed, they took refuge in a pub. Drinking was about the only habit of humans Death completely agreed with, well that and sleeping and having sex. It was the perfect way to mask one's troubles.

The three colleagues were a sorry sight to see. As they sat in the pub and drowned their sorrows, they watched the news, which was showing the discovery of Douglas' body. Death looked around the pub and Anne checked social media. Douglas' death did not seem to faze most people, for it was widely accepted that unless you were a Laskian, you were safe from Douglas Roach. There were quite a few jokes being made in the pub and online about Douglas, 'Hitler copycat' and 'they should have used a Russian' were the most popular. It was all quite distasteful and reminded Death of all the other leaders he had seen go down in a similar way over the centuries.

"Another round?" Mr Sharp asked.

"Yes, why not?" Death answered.

Mr Sharp went to the bar to get what Death hoped was the third round, but it was more likely the fourth or fifth.

"My wife is going to be so upset," Death said to Anne.

"It's not your fault, Mr D. You did exactly what you set out to do. Besides ten million is a substantial number."

"Not compared to eight billion."

"Well, you totally beat Hitler's documented number."

"It's not the same... there were less humans around in his day. When you adjust it for inflation, it's practically the same number," Death said, hanging his head.

"Oh, yeah, true... well, I'm sure we'll think of something else. We have all the time in the world," Anne said with a wink.

Death put his head in his hands. Mr Sharp came back with the drinks.

"So, have we come up with a new plan yet?" He asked, sitting down.

"No. I believe I shall just wallow in self-pity for a while," Death said as he took a swig of self-pity.

"Maybe we could start poisoning all the alcohol in the world? We could wipe out Australia and Ireland within weeks. Not to mention Scotland."

"Not a bad idea, Mr Sharp, but I could never do that to Scotch or Irish. I love it far too much."

"How about we only poison Bourbon then?" Mr Sharp said, grinning.

Death laughed. As a Scotch/Irish drinker, drinking Bourbon was almost a sin.

"Well, that should take care of all the rednecks," Anne added.

The three of them laughed.

"MR SHARP SUGGESTED that we poison all the bourbon in the world," Death said to his wife.

Death could feel her chuckle behind him as the bath water sloshed around them. Death was finally home and was in the company of his loving wife. She was attempting to consolidate him.

"The USA would be done for then."

"Yes, but I do love America. Their love for guns has been fantastic for business. I do hope they never amend that amendment."

The sounds of the wife's laugh filled Death's ears, and for a moment he forgot his troubles..

"You shouldn't worry too much, my love. I'm sure there will always be another dictator."

Death sighed in reply. Death's failure was still greatly irritating him. The wife wrapped her arms around her husband and squeezed.

"You were a mortal once, my dear. Please help me to understand these humans. Why do they complain about life yet fight so hard to keep on living? Why do they start wars and then pour so much time and effort into fighting illnesses? Their lack of consistency is exhausting. They expect Death to be on their terms - when they're ready. They have no concern for me at all."

"Oh, my love, you ask for logic where you will find none."

"Am I?"

"Yes. There is no soundness to humans. They are far too emotional to be rational creatures. They forever deny the laws of nature, the laws of anything really."

"I suppose I almost admire them for that."

"Unfortunately, my love, there is one aspect of humans that you have never been able to defeat. Something that even the greatest of evils has not been able to destroy."

Death turned to his wife. Was there going to be another thing Death would find hard to kill?

"Anne has already lectured me on my inability to conquer, defeat and kill love."

"No, my love. I am talking about hope. Humans are full of it."

There was another thing Death thought humans were full of, but he decided not to be vulgar. He gathered that hope was like love – another force that was not physical, but also very hard to destroy and could be rekindled at any moment. An added human aspect ever evading him. He blamed Mother Nature for this as he was sure it was something she had come up with.

Ob La Di, Ob La Da

True to form, it took about two months for the world to forget the last eight months. Now that the war had ended and the murders had stopped, the news consisted once more of petty crimes and sports results with the occasional segment on skinny polar bears and sea levels rising. The name Douglas Roach was slowly becoming a memory, and Urit was making it's amends to the Laskians and Laskia. It was heard a piece of land was to be gifted to the Laskians for all of them to live on in peace. Laskia was practically a wasteland now, and any remaining Laskians from around the world would never dare to live there. A new home was to be the answer. The land intended for the Laskians already had people living on it. However, it was presumed this would not be a problem, and the two peoples would happily live side by side once a border was established..

Things had returned to normal for Death and the team. The human world seemed to be back to its usual self. The Death numbers had slowed back to normal but overall, it had been Death's best year since nineteen forty-five. Mother Nature had even sent Death a card for his efforts. It was a picture of a monkey laughing. Death took it as a compliment.

Death had not immediately returned to work. Instead, he chose to take a vacation for a few weeks and spend time with his wife. Death and his wife took a holiday in Australia. Australia was Death's favourite vacation place for he rarely needed to make any effort there to achieve a result. It was a country Death encouraged all living things to go to at least once. Mother Nature had done a number on this land. If it wasn't the bushfires it was the floods. If it wasn't the hole in the ozone layer that gave everyone cancer it was the drought that killed all nature and animals. If it wasn't the poisonous snakes, it was the spiders.

Day after day, Death would lie on a beach in Perth and watch melanoma's form on the humans. Usually, this would give him great joy but he just felt like such a failure. He understood why Hitler saw suicide as his only way out. Sadly, Death was never going to be an option for himself. He was, and must always be, constant. He would never have the long sleep; he would never know peace.

"You know we can't stay here forever, right?" The wife said, lying next to Death on the sand.

Death sighed.

"I know."

"You must go back to work my love; you enjoy it far too much and are so good at what you do."

"Am I?"

"Of course."

Death stared off into the distance.

"What is it, my love?" She asked.

"I've been thinking lately, I'm not actually that good at my job, that I'm not even needed. I feel that the humans are running the show and they don't even know it!"

"You sound like you are having a mid-life crisis, my love. I thought that sort of thing only happened to living males."

Death pouted; this was not the reassurance he was after.

"But, I suppose it's a mid-death crisis for you," the wife said, grinning.

Death growled; he was pretty annoyed at how insensitive she was being. Mid-life or mid-death meant that he had made it halfway, but had he? Would he never not be around? Was 'mid' even a term for him?

"Help! Help! Help!"

A man was running out of the ocean with a woman in his arms. Blood surrounded them.

"She was attacked by a shark! Please help!"

Everyone on the beach except for the wife and Death ran over to help the couple. The woman was fading fast. She was losing a large amount of blood where the shark had bitten her on her leg. Death and his wife stayed as they were.

"I forgot about the sharks," the wife said.

A rush of warmth ran through Death.

"I do adore this country."

A mid-death crisis was avoided for now, or maybe Death would buy a sports car when they got home. Who knew?

DEATH WAS WALKING UP the stairs of headquarters when he felt a breeze of air go by him. It was the usual culprit running past him, attempting to be on time but constantly failing.

"Good morning, Aurora."

Aurora turned around in shock.

"Oh Mr D, sorry didn't see you there. I was just ahh..."

"Running late for work?" Death said with a smirk.

Aurora giggled.

"Why am I still in as much of a rush now as I was when I was alive?"

"That's death," Death said with a wink.

Aurora laughed as Death opened the door to headquarters for her.

"And I thought chivalry was dead."

Death and Aurora laughed; it was most certainly dead.

"Didn't you just get back from Australia?"

"Yes."

"How was it?"

"Lovely! Everywhere I looked, something wanted to kill you."

"Shouldn't you have a tan?"

"Why? Do I look as pale as a dead person?"

"Love your dad jokes, Mr D," Aurora said, rolling her eyes.

"Thank you, Aurora."

Aurora ran off, and Death went in the direction of his office. When he walked into the office, he found Anne and Mr Sharp watching the news. Mr Sharp was in his suit, Anne in her tight skirt with a stack of paperwork in her arms.

"Good morning Anne. Good morning Mr Sharp. What's so interesting in the news this morning?"

"Come over here and watch. We think you'll enjoy it," Anne said.

"Oh really? Why?"

Death walked over to them and looked at the TV. The reporter was talking about a virus that was slowly moving across the globe.

Death's stomach gave a flutter. This hope thing was not only for humans he was learning.

"I believe this can be good for us, Sir. I was looking at the figures late last night and noticed a huge spike in numbers due to this virus. You should call Mother Nature and find out how infectious it is and how good it might be for business. I estimate it will spread worldwide, not quite the Black Plague or the Spanish Influenza but good enough for modern times."

"Excellent idea Mr Sharp. I believe I will. It's about time that woman threw me a bone. I mean I do all this work for her for free."

"It's very ungrateful of her," Anne said in agreement.

Death and Mr Sharp nodded.

"So, is there a name for this virus yet?" Death asked.

"Something nineteen..."

The Not Quite End

"Those who can make you believe absurdities can make you commit atrocities."

- Voltaire

www.ingramcontent.com/pod-product-compliance
Lightning Source LLC
Chambersburg PA
CBHW020128180726
47992CB00020B/2546